The Final Page

THOMAS JOHN HOWARD BOGGIS

FIRST PRINTING, April 2022.
Harry Markos, Director.

Paperback: ISBN 978-1-914926-88-4
eBook: ISBN 978-1-914926-89-1

Book design by: Ian Sharman
Cover art by: Mark Gerrard
Editor: Stephen Davis

www.markosia.com

First Edition

PROLOGUE
The Nature of Chance

I have a question that has plagued me my whole life – *what makes us who we are?*

If the adventure I am about to relate has taught me anything, it is that our lives are a series of tests, and many of these tests come about by accident – so is it chance? Does chance propel us into these situations to test us – to see if we will sink or swim? Are these chance tests – and whether we succeed or fail – the way we forge our notion of self?

I will always wonder why I turned out the way I am. Or I should say the way I *was*… For a time, I was reminded of who I was on an almost daily basis. Their repeated taunts became a label, and although I tried to fight this label at first, I knew that there was some truth to it.

I was never what you would call an outgoing person. I didn't have many friends in my village. I rarely even bothered trying to fit in with the other children. I was different to them. They possessed a fearlessness that is afforded to only the very young – a veneer of bravery that is in fact a lack of experience.

Whatever I may call it, I did not possess it.

My mother called me a "worrier", and this was indeed one word for it, for everything made me nervous. Every situation I entered into had to be vetted for danger, for repercussions, and if there was even a hint of something wrong, I would immediately back away.

In her eyes I was a worrier, but the village children had perhaps a more apt word for it.

Coward.

I remember crystal clear the first time I was called this. I must have been seven or eight at the time. By chance I had stumbled across a group of village children while out for a walk and – against my better judgement – I joined them in a game of dares.

My usual tactic of simply keeping quiet and hoping to be forgotten about served me well at first until at last the group turned on me. It was *my turn*. A young girl, Elisa – who I secretly admired but had rarely spoken to – dared me to enter the abandoned house on the edge of the village.

This old house, which used to belong to the Francesco family, was now so old that it was literally falling to pieces. The house itself held a certain morbid allure for the village children.

Years ago, before any of us had been born, a boy was killed whilst exploring the upper floors. He had been ascending the stairs to the attic when the rotten wood had given way beneath him, plunging him three storeys to the cellar below.

This story had become the stuff of grisly legend. Ghost stories circulated amongst the village children. On cold, dark nights, they would say, when the moon is full, you can sometimes catch the sound of the stairs splintering below the boy and his last scream as he dropped out of this world.

For all the fear and mystery that surrounded the house, it was surprising how many children dared enter it. True, none of them would go upstairs, but a lot of them would creep cautiously through the front door before rushing out again, feeling very proud of themselves.

With this in mind my small group and I had approached the garden of the Francesco house. It was a bright, sunny day; there was not a cloud to be seen anywhere, yet somehow shadows clung to the building like a shroud.

We stood outside and already I began to feel the first gnawing tendrils of fear pulling at me, poking and prodding me; *find a way out of this, now!* I looked down at my feet, hoping to be swallowed up by the ground beneath me.

'Go on,' Elisa said, nudging me forward. 'All you have to do is walk through the front door. Go on!' She nudged me again and I stumbled forward.

My head was like a beehive, buzzing, buzzing, buzzing; anxieties and imagined dangers zipping back and forth.

My heart was pounding so hard it was like a fist in my chest, pummelling at my ribcage as if trying to escape. My feet were dead weights and felt as though they did not belong to me.

I shuffled slowly towards the front door, the buzzing growing louder and more frantic with every step until I began to feel light-headed. I wanted nothing more than to turn back, to give in to my fears, but Elisa was watching – how could I?

The building towered over me, blotting out the sun, the doorway ahead of me a portal to terror unknown. I reached the front steps and steadied myself on the hand rail. I tried to think rationally; this was just a house. Hundreds of children had entered it previously on dares just like this, and as long as I didn't go upstairs or jump up and down or anything I would be fine.

But this rational thinking was drowned by the buzzing. I couldn't do this. I had to get out of here, *now*. I turned and ran back down the garden path. As I pushed my way through the group Elisa shouted after me:

'You're a coward, William Belmont! A coward!'

I reached the corner of the street and turned, my breathing harsh and rasping. The buzzing was diminishing and my heart rate was slowing as I watched the other children rush giggling up the path and in through the front door of the Francesco house.

For a minute I could hear their muffled voices spilling out of the open door. Then they reappeared, running back down the path, laughing and shouting. I remembered thinking then, *What made me so different to them? Why were they able to do that when I was not?*

After that I spent even less time with the other children. I had nothing to say to them and they had only one thing to say to me. And I did not want to hear what I already knew.

Instead, most of my time was spent with my dog Milo, wandering the fields that surrounded our village. But Milo was weak after sustaining injuries from an incident I do not like to think about – let alone talk about – and our time together was fleeting.

After Milo died I wandered the fields alone, but that label stuck with me. Whenever the other children saw me they would call me it. *Coward.*

Thinking about it now, chance threw me into that situation, and I failed it. I sank. But the thing about chance is that it is prepared to give you a second shot.

Chance can make or break a life, a cosmic roll of the dice can decide whether a man lives or dies. And, as chance would have it, I, a coward, was chosen to perform a grand endeavour…

CHAPTER 1
The Impromptu Battleground

I don't know why this war started. To be honest I don't think it really matters. They can start for so many different reasons – religion, resources, greed – but the outcome for the innocent is always the same.

Fear.

I don't even know who struck first in this war. Some say the Kemalans to the west began it when they assassinated a high-ranking official in the Altegan government. Others say the Altegans started it when they crossed the Kemalan borders and began mining for metals and coal.

But, as I said, from our point of view it made no difference. We owed no allegiance to either side and being trapped between their two countries meant we suffered the brunt of their actions.

Fear became our whole lives. Fear of imminent attack, fear of groundless arrests and theft for the "war effort". Fear of fear itself. An underground network sprang up, a small group of brave men and women who would broadcast the locations of the armies as often as they could.

For this reason the wireless became our God. Its words could alleviate fear and doubt, if only for a little while, but its words could just as easily bring us to our knees.

We would listen to the reports on the wireless as often as they were made, praying that the fighting would take place anywhere but here. If we heard that their tanks and infantry were many miles away, we could go outdoors and for a few hours we could live our lives in some semblance of normality, before we returned to the wireless to see what our God's next words to us would be.

For me, at age fourteen, the change was not as dramatic as it was for the others in my village. I had lived my whole life in fear. Fear had dictated my every move up to this point. All I was seeing in these people now was a reflection of myself. A living mirror for how I had run my life.

But perhaps I am generalising. My parents were scared certainly, but they were among the few people who did not let fear control them. My father was an electrician, and while other families cowered in their kitchens, huddled around their wirelesses, he would visit their houses and make repairs. His strength of spirit was enough to keep hope alive in many hearts, but in even the most optimistic person it was nothing more than a dim glow.

Like my father, my mother was not someone you could keep down easily. She possessed a strength and bravery that I will never know. I remember her once telling me that fear is simply a state of mind and I remember thinking, *Of course it is, what a ridiculous thing to say. It's been the state of my mind for fourteen years.*

At the time I did not understand this nor did I try to. Fear was the only thing I knew, I had no weapons to combat it. Thinking about it now, however, I believe I know what she meant. Fear can only thrive if you allow it into your heart. If you open yourself up to fear it will gladly consume every inch of you like a raging inferno.

I had been open to fear my whole life but chance, it seems, was not happy for me to continue this way. By chance, an event occurred that thrust me down a path towards an end I could not have foreseen and I found myself, shocked and numb, walking down a dirt road surrounded by men, women and children from my village.

We had been walking for about an hour but to my leaden limbs it seemed far longer. No one was really saying much, but occasionally the silence was broken by a sob or a stifled grunt of pain.

The usual buzzing of fear and worry was dim and muffled, as though coming from very far away. As far away as it was, I knew it would sidle back sooner or later, so for now I simply savoured the void it left behind.

Although I could not feel it myself, I could taste the fear on the air. The war had finally reached us for real and it had wasted no time in making its presence known. We had been completely unprepared. In fact, no one had been prepared for what occurred.

I glanced around at all the pain and grief-stricken faces and saw many I recognised. Some, like Elisa, who I would rather not have seen, but I also noticed – with a dull feeling of sadness – the absence of several faces I had once known.

I lifted my hand from the crook of my right arm and watched a trickle of blood flow down my clothing and fall to the road. The wound was not severe, but it hurt like hell. A woman walking next to me, who I recognised as the owner of a small grocery stall in the village, noticed the injury. Without saying anything, she tore a strip off her ragged clothing and bandaged the wound carefully. When she was done, she flashed me a weak smile.

'You'll live, son,' she said.

I tried to smile back but I could not muster up much more than a twitch at the edge of my mouth. I looked down at the female collie walking along faithfully by my side. Ada. The one remotely good thing to come out of this. She looked up at me with her loyal brown eyes then flicked an ear towards a sound coming from my right.

A soldier marched into view, the rattle of his grenade pins sounding on every fall of his heavy boots, his N19 carbine rifle held alert and steady, ready to take a life at a moment's notice.

I could not tell what side he was on until I overheard one of the villagers say that they were

Kemalan. This made sense as they were marching us west, presumably to one of their prison camps.

The mere thought of this was enough to make my heart skip a beat. I had heard rumours of these camps and the rumours were not pretty. Supposedly, at night, prisoners were shepherded into small pens – generally too many for comfort – and given little food and poor lavatory facilities.

During the day, from sunrise to sunset, prisoners were forced to aid with the war effort, building roads and bridges, weapons and vehicles; whatever was required at that particular time. If you were too old or too weak you were put to work mending uniforms or in the mess hall serving food.

From what I had heard, prisoners were also indoctrinated during their imprisonment. After work, whilst crammed into their pens, they would be shown Kemalan news footage, detailing how "our boys" were "winning the war", and they would be given speeches from high ranking officials on how greatly their efforts were appreciated.

Perhaps these rumours were just that. Or perhaps everything I'd heard was true. Or perhaps they stemmed from truth but were greatly exaggerated. I did not know, but it was looking increasingly likely that I was going to find out.

The guard noticed me staring at him and frowned, flicking his head at me dismissively.

'What are you looking at, boy?' he grunted. I turned away quickly and my eyes fell on another guard walking to the left of the group. I felt my world close ever tighter around me. We were penned in; sheep being led by shepherds.

So this was it. My life was over already. It had happened so quickly and so recently that I had not been able to process any of it yet. I tried to arrange my thoughts and work through it. Maybe if I could understand it better it would make the pain easier to bear.

It had happened only last night. My parents and I had been walking home from the neighbouring town. We had just stocked up on supplies, an endeavour that we could only undertake on very rare occasions. As usual our God, the wireless, had informed us that the armies were elsewhere, well away from our village, and we had taken the opportunity to hurry and purchase things we were running low on.

The fear in the village was so great that my parents had even agreed to pick up supplies for several other families. This is why they had brought me along. Normally my fears would have kept me rooted to my chair in the kitchen, just like all the other families, but today my father needed me to help carry things. I loved and respected my father and I did not want to let him down, so I had agreed to go, even as the buzzing screamed at me to stay.

And so, weighted down with supplies, we had staggered home southwards across the fields. Night had begun to fall and up ahead I could make out the weak glow of the lamps that lined our village streets. The silence all around us was deep and impenetrable and for a moment it felt like there was no one in the world but us.

I had always been afraid of the dark, ashamed as I am to say it, and so I kept close to my father's side as we entered the outskirts of the village and turned towards home.

A sound away to the west disturbed the silence and my father stopped suddenly, causing me to bump into him.

'What is it?' my mother asked, looking concerned. 'What did you hear?'

'I could have sworn I heard... but it could have just been...'

'What?' she persisted. 'What did it sound like?'

'It sounded like a rifle being cocked,' my father answered.

Tense and alert, they glanced all around us, listening for any further sounds. When none were forthcoming, my mother began to move once again.

'Come on,' she said, chivvying me along. 'Let's get home. Hurry up now, Will.' As I quickened my pace, fear began to bubble below the surface once more.

'Do you think it could be..?' I tried to ask, but my father cut across me.

'I'm sure it's nothing, Will,' he said quickly. 'Just stay calm – we'll be alright.'

We hurried onwards, my hearing suddenly seeming a hundred times amplified. Every tiny sound became the footfall of an enemy soldier; every breath of wind was the passage of a bullet narrowly missing me.

The streetlamps cast vague circles of light across the cobbles that only served to emphasise the darkness outside their perimeters. I was looking ahead, towards one such circle of light, when I spotted a silhouetted figure pass by it.

'Did you see...?'

'Hush, Will,' my father said, his voice barely audible.

We had finally reached the end of our street and were just turning into it when a sound close by made us stop in our tracks. We ducked down behind a low wall and looked out across a series of neat back gardens. I was so close to my father that I felt his body tense at the sight before us.

Soldiers.

Men in full combat gear and carrying rifles were quietly scrambling over the fences at the rear of the gardens, heading east. Towards our home.

I could not count how many there were. My fear was growing, rushing towards my psyche like a tidal wave whilst my father continued to stare at them, sizing up the situation.

'We must go back,' he said at last, so quietly I could barely catch it. 'It's not safe here. Follow...' Before he could finish his sentence he had turned to look back the way we had come and realised that we were trapped.

Soldiers were approaching along the street, keeping out of the light, their weapons raised as they swept the area for threats. They moved in tight formation, covering every angle – a well-oiled killing machine, drilled to perfection.

So disciplined were their movements that their boots made hardly any sound on the cobbled road and I realised that they would have been on top of us before we had even known they were there.

A sudden shrill yell nearby made them drop to the ground, their rifles raking the streets for signs of a threat.

'They're here! They're here! Open fire!'

Gunfire exploded in the silence, the rattle of machineguns shredding the peace. My father pushed me down into the shadows, his head flicking back and forth as he searched for immediate danger.

Paralysed by fear, I watched as one of the soldiers nearby stood up and began to gesticulate to his men.

'Alpha team, on me! Charlie team, secure the perimeter! Do not let anyone past you!'

'Yes, sir!' they barked back as the group split in two, one hurrying off down our street and the other remaining where they were, blocking our only escape route. Chances are they would have let us by, once they realised we were not enemy combatants, but chances were just as high they would have shot us as soon as they spotted movement.

My father clearly believed that the latter was most likely.

'We have to get to the cellar,' he yelled over the gunshots. 'It's our safest bet now. Stay in the shadows and follow me.' He grabbed my hand, crouched low and began to lead the way home. As he pulled me along I reached back and grasped my mother's hand, taking comfort from her touch.

Hand in hand, we hurried down the street. We stayed low and kept out of the light, taking cover behind objects wherever possible. Soldiers passed by us, unaware of our presence, their gunfire deafeningly loud.

I stumbled once or twice on the uneven ground, but my father's grip on my hand was firm and he did not let me fall. Without him I think I would have stopped where I was, too terrified to move or even think.

I had walked down this street so many times. I had known fear here before, but it was the same fear I had known all my life. This was different. This was overwhelming. This was unlike anything I had ever dreamed of.

We were passing a side street as an explosion went off at the far end, gouging a huge chunk out of the cobbles. Rubble kicked up by the blast reached us even here, zipping past as dust showered down on top of us.

'Was that a grenade? A mortar?' I managed to ask breathlessly over the din, but my father did not answer.

Our house came into view at last, a haven of safety amidst the storm. Bullets suddenly ripped into the wall by my head and I threw up my arms to protect my face. I looked back to see a soldier falling to the floor, his weapon discharging wildly as he died.

Dashing ahead, my father barged through our back gate and held it open. I followed my mother as she rushed into the garden and ran for the trap door leading to the cellar. Slamming the gate behind him, my father sprinted ahead of us and slid back the bolt, ushering us inside. Once we were safely within he scanned the area for threats one last time before shutting and locking the doors.

Our breathing sounded abnormally loud in the confined space as I slumped down against a wall and drew my knees up under my chin. My father hurried to a cupboard and pulled out a candle and box of matches. He lit the candle and set it down on a packing case beside us.

With nowhere to go, my parents sat down on either side of me and held me close. My body was shaking with fear, but I drew strength from the steady and stoic presence of my father, who throughout all this had remained cool and level-headed.

I think that is the thing I will remember most about him. He was so much stronger than I was. I often wonder whether he was ashamed to have me as a son. I would not have blamed him if he had been. I am ashamed now of how I was back then.

A series of explosions impacted like a drum roll overhead. The ground shook, dust and rubble rained down and the sound of crumbling masonry reached our ears. Gunfire and screams echoed through the streets and I looked up at the sound of heavy footfalls on the ceiling above us.

They were in our house.

I shuffled closer to my father and he hugged me tight. As we sat there, looking upwards like stargazers, the one cogent thought running through my head was, *don't let them find us. Don't let them come down here…*

My throat was parched and a lump the size of a tennis ball seemed to be lodged there. I tried to speak but could manage nothing more than a croak. A jug of water stood on a workbench nearby and my mother stood up carefully and retrieved it, passing it across to me.

I held the jug to my lips and took a long draft, my hands shaking so badly that water slopped all over my chin and clothes. I offered the jug to my father and he took a swift drink before passing it along to my mother.

'What will happen to us?' I managed to choke through my fear. 'What will they do if they find us?' I could see in his eyes that my father was planning to lie to me, to sugar-coat the truth. It was the automatic response of any parent in such a situation. But in this case he could not bring himself to do it. His face changed and he decided to treat me like the man I should be.

'If they find us they will take us prisoner,' my father replied gravely. 'They will herd us together and lead us off to a prison camp. We will be penned in like cattle and forced to work to forward their efforts.' My eyes widened in shock and for a second I would almost have preferred the lie.

'They will take us prisoner, but they will not harm us,' my father continued. 'We are no use to them dead. Dead men cannot work.' My mother touched me gently on the shoulder and I turned to look at her.

'No matter what they do to us we will always have each other,' she said. 'That is something they cannot take away from us. Not now, not ever.'

More footsteps sounded overhead, gunfire boomed and the metallic *thunk* of mortar fire melded into the cacophony.

My father got to his knees and took my face in his hands, his steady brown eyes looking deep into my own.

'There's one thing I want you to remember, son,' he said, and as he said it I saw his eyes become moist in the weak candlelight. 'Do not let fear control you. Whatever else may happen in your life, I want you to remember this. *Do not let it* – promise me!'

I looked up into his eyes as tears filled my own. I had just opened my mouth to respond when an explosion rocked the building above us and the soldiers taking refuge there yelled in fear as our home began to collapse on top of them. With a deafening roar, the roof crashed down through the first floor and collided with the ceiling over our heads.

Huge chunks of wood, rubble and masonry punched through and fell towards us. Without thinking – and as though of one mind – my mother and father threw themselves on top of me, shielding me from the debris that rained down and pummelled them mercilessly.

Trapped beneath my parents I felt every impact through their bodies, until one particularly violent jolt cracked my head against the stone floor, and my world went black.

I will always remember that cellar. A large part of me died down there amongst the dirt and rubble. After extricating myself from the debris I sat there, groggy and disoriented, and stared at my parents blankly, unseeingly.

I felt strange, disconnected, as though I was looking at myself from outside my body. I saw the scene before me as you might see the reflection on a windswept pond; the same... but different, broken.

My head was pounding fit to burst but a steady numbness was also spreading from the wound at the back of my skull. I looked down at my right arm and saw that it was bleeding profusely.

Unsteady on my feet, I staggered up the cellar stairs and witnessed the true devastation of my home. There was little left. A hurricane had passed through this house and its name was war.

I bent down gingerly and lifted a burnt and torn photograph from beneath a section of door. The picture was one of the few we had and depicted me and my parents at a festival in the nearby town. It was torn almost in two and my face was all but indistinguishable, but I slipped it into my pocket anyway.

It was early morning and though I squinted, the sun's first rays pierced my eyelids, sending further waves of pain through my head. I threw up a hand to shield my eyes and noticed for the first time the other survivors milling around in the ruins of our former home. I also noticed the soldiers.

They were armed and stood in a rough cordon around my fellow villagers. Many of them were wounded and all of them looked battle-weary.

The scene all around them was one of devastation. Bodies littered the streets and empty shell casings lay everywhere like fallen leaves. Chunks of stone and masonry had been stacked haphazardly to form cover and mortar fire had punched jagged holes the full length of the street.

As though they had been waiting for me to emerge, the commander of the unit signalled to his men and they began to organise us, marshalling us into one group. No one argued. No one said anything.

Mutely, we were marched off down the road. I was too shocked and dazed to do anything other than follow the group, my mind blank, my hand pressed tightly against my wound.

As we walked, a sound close by filtered through to my damaged subconscious. A low whine was emanating from one of the buildings bordering the road. Without stopping, without pausing to contemplate the danger, I left the group and entered the building.

A soldier yelled at me to stop, but I ignored him. Inside, the house was a wreck. The west wall had fallen in and a section of the first floor had collapsed.

The whining grew louder as I drew close to an old dresser, tipped onto its side.

Beneath the dresser I saw a dog, pinned down, struggling to breathe. I hurried over and lifted the dresser, but try as I might I could not raise it more than a few inches. It was enough.

The dog crawled out on her belly and spun round to face me, tongue lolling, eager to please. She was a female collie, almost full grown, and when I bent to check I saw that she did not have a collar.

She licked my face as I stroked her ears, a name coming to me in a flash. *Ada*.

The soldier rushed into the room and stared at me in surprise. He opened his mouth to say something then seemed to change tack halfway through.

'That your dog?' he asked.

'No,' I replied simply, as Ada continued to lick my face. The soldier shook his head and waved his gun at me.

'Anyway, get back with the group – no one's allowed to wander off.'

'Why?' I asked quietly. The soldier looked nonplussed for a second.

'Just get back to the group, I won't ask again, boy.'

With Ada by my side I was led back to the group and we continued our westward march.

Chance had brought me to this place. Chance had determined that I would end up here, surrounded by the survivors of a terrible conflict. Chance had brought two armies unwittingly together on a cold, dark night – their field of battle a small, defenceless town.

Neither side had known of the other's movements. I later discovered that the Kemalans had been making a sweep of their border while the Altegans had been making a push west. Neither side had even known we were there, so small was our village that it did not appear on any maps.

Their meeting was the product of chance and the coercion of my first steps down a new path. But at that time I could not see the path before me. But I felt sure I could see its end – a prison camp...

CHAPTER 2
The Diary

Only an hour and a half had passed since I had left Chotolo – my home town – but it already seemed like an aeon ago. It was like recalling a story I had heard about someone else's life.

After thinking through the events that had led me here I realised that it had in fact made me feel a little better. I began to notice some clarity return to my thoughts. But with this clarity came a familiar feeling. Fear.

It reared its head like an old enemy – a cunning, ruthless foe that knew all my weaknesses and just how to manipulate them to control my actions. The stoic exterior I had exhibited – born of numbness and shock – was fast crumbling around me and I became the scared little boy I remembered from the story I had just recalled.

I reached down and buried my hand in the scruff of Ada's neck, drawing comfort from her warmth, but I suddenly felt very small once again – and very alone. Of their own accord, my legs ceased all movement and I stopped abruptly in the middle of the road.

The man walking behind me stumbled and almost fell. He spun around to look at me and his eyes widened in recognition.

'Is that you, Will?' he asked. In the same instant I realised who he was. His name was Anthony Bellini. He was a painter and decorator who had been good friends with my father. They had often worked together and he and his family had come round to dinner on a couple of occasions.

He had a son, Oscar, who was one of the few children who did not taunt me on a regular basis. That may have been because Oscar was often the brunt of jeers himself, but that didn't stop any of the other bullied children. They would all turn on me if they thought they could save face. I was fair game to all…

When I did not answer, Anthony looked around us hurriedly and gripped me by the shoulders, gently but firmly easing me back into a fast walk.

'Don't want to do anything to stand out, son,' he said, glaring at one of the soldiers walking nearby. 'There's no telling what they might do.'

I looked up at him and tried to think of something to say, but even with everything that had happened, nothing was forthcoming. I always found it difficult to talk to adults.

When I said nothing, Anthony took over the questioning.

'Will, where's your father?' he asked, looking at me seriously. 'Your mother? I haven't seen them anywhere.'

I tried to tell him what happened, but I could not bring myself to say it. In my mind's eye I had already relived that event once, and I could not bring myself to say it out loud.

As silly as it sounds, it felt like it would only become real if I spoke the words. If I shared my story it would become fixed, indelible, but as it was, the story was mine alone and while it remained mine it was only as real and as true as I wanted it to be. And I wanted so badly for it not to be true.

'Back there,' I said quietly, pointing vaguely behind us.

'At the back of the group you mean?' Anthony asked, momentarily brightening up. He had clearly been expecting the worst.

'No, back there, in Chotolo… at home…' I trailed off. I could not say any more than that. If I left it like that then they were just at home, sleeping, and I could return one day and wake them.

His face fell but he recovered it quickly, tightening his grip on my shoulder in a reassuring way.

'It's ok, son,' he said. 'I understand.'

For several minutes we walked on in silence, both of us wrapped up in our own private thoughts. The mood of the people around me was weighing heavily on my spirit, trampling it down further than I ever thought it could get.

This is what it feels like to have your freedom taken from you, I thought. *This is what it feels like to know there is no happiness left in your future. This is what war does to people.*

I looked at one of the soldiers flanking us with a sudden flash of hatred and my hands unconsciously balled into fists. For a moment the fear was gone and all that was left was anger. They had taken everything from me, and still they wanted more.

Walking beside me, Anthony noticed the tension in my shoulders and followed it down my arms to the fists swinging stiffly at my sides. He placed a hand gently on my arm and I glanced across at him.

'I know how you feel, Will,' he said in an undertone. 'But it's not worth it.'

'You don't have any idea how I feel,' I hissed back, surprising even myself.

'Oh I do, son,' he replied sadly. 'More than you know.' His expression spoke of hardships unvoiced for many years and for the first time I noticed the numerous lines that etched his face. He had been on this earth far longer than I and my retort suddenly felt very silly.

My thoughts flew to my father and I remembered that he and Anthony were... or should I say *had been*... the same age. Strangely though, whenever I had looked at my father I had not seen the lines criss-crossing his face. To me he had been ageless – but isn't that always the way with parents?

When we are young we do not see them as creatures that age. We do not see them in the same way we view other people. They are our constants, our bedrocks; the mere thought of life without them is incomprehensible to us. To children, parents do not age and in their minds they will always be there.

My hands relaxed as my thoughts returned and, when Anthony was satisfied I would not do something stupid, he released my arm.

'I know how you feel, Will,' he continued, 'because this is not my first war. Take a look over there.' He pointed towards an odd looking structure buried within a hillside to the north of the road.

At first I had no idea what it was, then I got a clearer look at it. It was a bunker. Covered in moss and riddled with cracks and bullet holes, it looked out westwards, guarding the road from attack. It was a desolate, lonely place, with nothing but the road to see for miles around. I pitied the poor souls who had been stationed here, alone, miles from civilisation. If they were to die in that place it would not be known about for days.

And many men had died here, I did not have to be a psychic to know that. I could picture the scene as clear as day:

Soldiers marching unaware down the darkened road, scouting the area ahead, sticking to the drainage ditches to minimise the risk of detection. Weapons raised, nerves jangling, alert for the slightest sound.

From within the bunker, a weapon's crosshair finds them and a deafening cacophony of shots rings out in the night. The soldiers fall dead, their bodies rolling limply into the ditch.

The weapon withdraws inside the bunker, the occupant now off his guard, unaware that he has been flanked.

A yell of shock, suddenly cut short, echoes briefly across the fields as muzzle flare lights up the inside of the bunker, the shots resounding hollowly off the concrete walls. A body slumps to the floor, never to rise again.

The last man standing checks the bodies of his dead comrades before continuing down the road, leaving behind him an eerie stillness.

I shook the image from my mind as Anthony's words stirred up memories of my history lessons. This was not the first time our land had been ravaged by war. The first Grand War had taken place around forty years ago, and what a conflict it had been. Hundreds of thousands of soldiers had been marched to their deaths and around a million civilians had been caught in the crossfire.

Last time, many nations had joined forces to rid the world of the oppression and tyranny of one country, whose ambitions had ultimately outweighed their reach. With their disarmament and removal as a global power, the world was made a safer place. But the cost of war had been too high and after, at the behest of their people, most nations wanted no further hand in war.

That is, of course, unless the war was brought to them.

For that reason, the war I now found myself in went unheeded by the wider world. It did not affect them; not their material interests nor their people, so why should they intervene? Even as innocent civilians met their maker at the hands of the vicious war machine, the rest of the world simply turned a blind eye, and ignored it.

I looked away from the bunker as Anthony sighed, long and low.

'My uncle was drafted into the army during the first Grand War,' he said. 'Our country wasn't involved; we were caught between the two sides, just like now, but they forced him to join up and set him to guard that bunker right there.' His eyes remained fixed on the bunker as he spoke.

'He never left it,' Anthony finished, finally breaking eye contact with the lonely structure. I bowed my head and could not bring myself to look at him as I spoke.

'I'm sorry,' I murmured. 'Sorry for what I said before.'

'That's ok, son,' Anthony replied. 'You weren't to know.'

It was nearing noon and the sun was riding high in a cloudless blue sky; a perfect day that seemed to mock our hopeless situation. The air around me was heavy with sweat and clouds of dust kicked up by the people walking ahead made me splutter and choke. Flies droned around our heads, drawn by the smell.

By this point I was flagging badly. I needed water. I needed to rest. But our captors were relentless, marching us ceaselessly onwards. They did not seem to get tired, or perhaps they were simply trained not to show it. Every now and then I would spot them drinking from their hip flasks, and this only made me hate them even more.

Anthony had returned to his family. He had asked me to join them but I had politely declined, saying that I needed to be alone for a while. He had persisted, but in the end he relented when I said I would join them by the end of the day.

My clothes were sticking to me uncomfortably and I was beginning to feel light-headed when I spotted a disturbance up ahead. The group seemed to be shuffling to the left of the road, giving something a wide berth. Gasps and muffled exclamations reached my ears and I stood on tiptoes to try and get a look at the source, but I could not see anything over the throng of people.

Ada cocked her head at the sudden commotion but stayed firmly by my side, her ears flicking back and forth. I began to force my way to the far right of the group to get a better look. When I broke through I saw that the road was bordered by a deep, wide drainage ditch. At first I could not spot what had caused the disturbance. Then I saw it.

A body lay by the side of the road. Only the feet were visible over the lip of the ditch, but I could see the flies zipping back and forth. Even from here, the smell was horrendous and I was forced to cover my mouth with my hand. I was repulsed by the sight and fear rushed through me like an electric current, but I could not tear my eyes away.

Without considering the consequences, I broke from the group and – with Ada by my side – ran towards the body. Luckily, the soldiers flanking our group were not looking at the time or this story could have ended very quickly.

I reached the edge of the ditch and skidded to a halt. There was not one body there but several. Five men in all lay dead in that ditch, their bodies strewn haphazardly, left where they fell. Filthy water surrounded their bodies, their blood staining it a deep crimson. I noticed in horror that each man had a bullet hole in his forehead and realised that they had been executed.

The men did not look like soldiers, so what had they done that had resulted in their executions? Were they murderers? Thieves? More than likely their only crime was being in the wrong place at the wrong time. They stared sightlessly up at me and I almost wept – this was no way for a life to end.

I scanned the grisly scene and was about to turn away when – by chance – a gust of wind blew along the ditch, lifting the hem of a dead man's jacket to reveal an object buried in the mud at his side. It appeared to be some kind of book, but its title was illegible due to a boot print stamped on top of it.

'Hey!' One of the soldiers had finally noticed what I was up to and started to run towards me. I reached down quickly and dug the book out of the mud. With my sleeve I wiped away the worst of the dirt and grime and was able to read the title.

The lettering was embossed and personalised. It read: "The Diary of Isabella Bertolli." The soldier was almost on top of me. Without thinking, I thrust the diary inside my coat and turned to meet him.

'What the hell do you think you're doing!' the soldier yelled. Then he realised who I was and I realised who he was. It was the same soldier who had chased me into the house when I rescued Ada.

'Oh, it's you again,' he said and, strangely, his tone softened as he said it. 'What were you doing?'

'I… I couldn't help myself,' I replied. 'I had to have a look.' The soldier looked past me into the ditch and frowned. Then his face changed and he moved in closer, whispering conspiratorially to me.

'You've got to stay with the group, boy,' he said. 'You've got to, or I'll be forced to do something I really don't want to do.'

I nodded my understanding then quietly, meekly, returned to the group with Ada walking obediently alongside me. Many of my fellow prisoners looked at me oddly as I re-entered their ranks, but I ignored them. My thoughts were focussed upon one thing and one thing only… the diary.

Furtively, I checked all around to make sure that none of the guards were looking. They weren't – the coast was clear. I reached inside my coat and drew out the diary. My fingers unconsciously traced the embossed lettering as I inspected it. The cover was made of thick, black leather with gold-plated edging and the pages were gilded in gold. It looked well used, but also lovingly cared for. I could tell at once that this was a treasured item and it led me to wonder, what on earth was it doing in that ditch, surrounded by dead bodies?

If the name on the front cover was to be believed then this book belonged to a girl, one Isabella Bertolli, but I did not see any girls among the dead. Had one of those men stolen it and dropped it as they were executed? Was it coincidence that it ended up there? Perhaps Isabella had been marched past there just as I had and the diary had simply fallen from her grasp by mistake?

At the time I had no idea how the diary had ended up there and no idea where it would lead me, but I felt compelled to do something I would never normally do. I checked around once more – to make sure no one was looking – then I opened the diary and began to flick through it.

I had been raised by my parents to never pry into other people's affairs and personal property, but I knew right then that in this instance it was forgivable, for I had stumbled upon something greater than myself. As I rapidly skimmed through the diary a story began to unfold before me that set my heart racing and made me want to weep with pity.

The diary was indeed written by an Isabella Bertolli who, I soon discovered, was born and raised in a small village called Valania, many miles to the east of my village. I was only able to skim-read the diary in small snatches as we trudged along, for fear of being spotted by the guards and having it confiscated. Thus, the full details of her life were lost on me, but what I did discover – at least in part – was where she might be now.

It appeared that she and her family had been taken prisoner in their village by Kemalan soldiers – just as I had been – and were being led off westwards to the Kemalan HQ in Scioli. I searched for entries that would lift my spirits and give me hope, but the picture she painted was one of sorrow and hardship. Hastily scribbled phrases swam before my eyes, *"screams and yells"*, *"freedom taken away"*, *"no food or water"*, *"babies crying"*. The more I read, the more my heart went out to her. I wanted nothing more than to find some way to help her, but what could I possibly do?

Then it came to me.

I am not an impulsive person by nature. To be impulsive is to make snap decisions without fear, and that is not something I ever thought I was capable of. Every decision I have ever made has been influenced or driven by fear. This time it was different. I knew what I had to do and I was more certain of this fact than I had ever been about anything in my entire life.

I had to return the diary to Isabella.

There it was. The instant the thought entered my head it became as permanent and immovable as a mountain. I had set a task for myself and I knew right then there would be no backing down from it. This was something I would see through to the end; no matter how terrifying the task became, I would finish it.

For many years I had been branded a coward, and since that day outside the Francesco house – when I had first been called it – my actions had lived up to that title. I had been a coward. I had lived my life in fear and in so doing had barely lived at all. But a person can change. I did not have to remain a coward. All it would take would be the willingness to make that change, and the tenacity to carry it through.

I knew I could do this. I had to.

In order to pull this off I knew I would first have to make my escape, and to do that I would have to wait for nightfall. The guards were harsh taskmasters, but I was almost certain they would not make us march when we could not see. Once we'd made camp I would just have to pick my moment to slip away into the night.

It was early afternoon and there were still many hours of walking ahead of me. With my decision made I decided the best thing to do was to read the diary in-depth to see if I could glean any more useful information from it. Before doing so I pushed my way to the centre of the group – away from the beady eyes of the soldiers – and beckoned for Ada to follow me.

Thus hidden, I opened the diary to the first entry and began to read.

CHAPTER 3
Isabella's Story: Part 1

July 21st 1942

I love waking up in the morning. Most people, upon awaking and realising that they must get up and greet the new day, are grumpy and surly and want nothing more than to go back to sleep. They growl and they grunt and they resent the need to extricate themselves from their warm cocoons. But not me.

As I write this I am sitting on my bed and looking out of my bedroom window. I have become so used to writing now that I can chronicle my life almost without thinking, without looking even, which is good because my attention is focussed on the view outside. It is a glorious morning. The sun is shining brightly through the latticed glass and painting little glowing squares on my bed sheets. When I stretch my hand into the shafts of light I can feel the sun's warmth caressing my fingers and it makes me glad to be alive.

From across the farmyard I can hear the dairy cows lowing and it brings a smile to my face.

Whenever my friends come over to stay the night they always complain that those sounds keep them awake, but they have never bothered me. In fact, I find them comforting. I am so used to them that without them I might not be able to sleep at all.

Through the window I see my father walking to the cattle shed. He has a bucket in each hand, ready to begin the morning's milking. I knock loudly on the glass and he looks up, shielding his eyes against the glare of the early morning sun. He finally spots me and waves in greeting, his face splitting into that big smile I love so much.

I giggle as I notice his tousled hair – he has never been able to tame it, no matter how hard he tries. Right now it is sticking up in all directions, as though it is trying to leap from his head. His jaw too is covered in short but wild hair. My mother has been trying to get him to shave it off for weeks, but he likes it and I do too – it tickles when he kisses my cheek.

He says something but I cannot hear it through the glass. I can guess what it was though:

'Want to join me on my delivery to town this morning, Isabella?'

He asks me this every morning, but I have not accompanied him for a while now. Perhaps I will go with him on his next delivery.

July 22nd 1942

I am sitting in the kitchen watching my mother prepare breakfast. There is something very calming about watching her cook. She is so self-assured, so in control – I think this kitchen is the place I feel safest in the whole world. It is warm, quiet and secure (the walls are thick, there is only one window above the sink and the door to the yard is strong and double-bolted).

If ever I get scared or feel anxious or ill, I come here and somehow it makes me feel a little better. In the end I suppose it is just a room, of course it has no supernatural powers, but I'm sure everyone has a place like this. A place you retreat to when times are hard. A place you think of when you are far away and encounter trouble. A place where you feel comfortable, peaceful and protected, but most of all… loved.

My mother checks the eggs frying on the stove and slices up the last of a loaf of bread, then returns to kneading some dough for a fresh batch. She wipes the back of her hand across her forehead, leaving behind a floury smear. I stifle a laugh and she turns to look at me crossly.

'What's so funny young lady?' she asks me.

'Nothing,' I reply. She turns to look out of the window, still faintly suspicious, and catches sight of her reflection in the glass. She raises a hand to her forehead and rubs away some of the flour.

'So that's it, eh?' she asks in mock fury, unable to hide the bubble of laughter welling up inside her. She spins around to face me. 'I've heard that flour on the forehead brings good luck, want to try it?' She dips her hand into the bag of flour and begins to advance towards me, her shoulders shaking with mirth. For now, I think I will end this diary entry here!

July 23rd 1942

I had planned to go with my father on his delivery yesterday, but after being chased out of the kitchen by my mother and her flour-caked hand, I had instead gone to the stables and ridden my horse all morning. After forgetting again, I had resolved this morning to accompany my father. So here I am!

I am in the milk cart with my father on our way into town. Our faithful old carthorse Bessie is plodding along ahead of us, bearing us forth with enough milk to supply the town's inhabitants for another day. I have often wondered why my father does not buy a car. It would be much faster – his deliveries would only take a couple of hours rather than all morning. If I know my father like I think I know him then I already know the answer.

My father does not like modern technology, and he does not like change. His family have been dairy farmers for as long as he can remember. He is one of those people you would term as "set in their ways". This does not bother me, I am happy with our rustic lifestyle and do not envy my friends for the commodities they have that I do not.

For instance, several of my (admittedly wealthy) friends have these new "television sets". I have seen them and I do not understand what all the fuss is about. I tried to watch one of the pictures they showed and I found that it made my head hurt. Why would people want to sit inside in front of a box when they could go outside in the fresh air? Personally, I would much rather sit writing in my journal than slouch glassy-eyed in front of a flickering contraption. But I digress.

My father believes in a simple way of life and it is a belief that I share wholeheartedly. I must admit, only to you of course, that the prospect of staying here all my life and carrying on my father's work does not exactly thrill me, but I do know that wherever my life takes me, who I am will not be defined by things, but *deeds*.

I have not told this to anyone, but what I want more than anything is to pursue my writing into later life. I want my words to be read by millions of people. I want my thoughts and ideas to inspire, reassure and excite. I want more than anything to leave an indelible mark on this world and its inhabitants.

It seems silly and improbable, I know. It is fine to wish for such fanciful things, but making them happen is another matter entirely. For now, I am just a young girl living in a small town most people have never even heard of. Getting my words out to millions of people? That is something that will take some time. But then… I do have my whole life ahead of me. Who's to know what it will hold for me?

We are nearing the bridge into town. The spire of the church is visible in the distance behind the rooftops, its bells tolling the hour. Plumes of smoke are drifting lazily across the town from the textile mill on the northern outskirts. As we ascend onto the humped bridge – Bessie straining at her harness – I look down into the river below and spot a fish darting between patches of light and shadow. It is so hot I wish I could jump in there and join it.

As we enter the town itself I notice a group of my friends heading to the sweet shop and I give my father my best and most beguiling look. He knows I am teasing him and he laughs as he tells me to go off and enjoy myself. I will end this entry here; the eating of sweets must take precedence!

July 25th 1942

You would not believe the day I had yesterday. I have only just recovered from it myself. I was awoken, very early in the morning, by my father shouting for my mother. At first I could not understand what he was saying to her. All I knew was that whatever it was, it sounded urgent. I leapt out of bed and dressed quickly, then ran downstairs to find out what was going on.

I found my mother and father standing in the farmyard. They seemed worried and were looking at the stables as they spoke in hushed voices. When they saw me approach my father seemed to become more worried still, but then his face softened and he beckoned me close.

'I'm sorry to say this, Isabella,' he said gently, 'but it looks like Bessie has escaped.' I pulled away from him as I looked up in shock.

'Escaped? How?' I asked.

'We're not sure…' he replied. 'You did…' he struggled with the words. 'You did remember to shut the stable door firmly last night, didn't you?'

'Yes… I did,' I answered falteringly. 'At least… I think I did…' My father looked into my face, but there was no blame in his eyes.

'Well, it doesn't matter,' he said. 'Thing is, it's too dark to go looking for her now, we'll have to wait for sun-up to start searching.'

'What if she gets lost or hurt?' I asked, fear getting the best of me.

'She'll be alright, I doubt she's gone far,' he replied reassuringly. 'She's a tough'un, that horse, don't you worry about her.'

The following few hours were awful. None of us could sleep, though in truth we didn't exactly try very hard. I kept thinking about Bessie, alone out there in the dark. To anyone else she might be just a horse, but to us she is a member of the family. Perhaps it is just another part of our "rustic" lifestyle. I am quite sure none of my friends are as attached to their animals.

So I lay there on my bed looking out of the window, watching the darkness being driven away by the pale light appearing over the horizon. In my mind I ran over all the places nearby Bessie might have gone to: the stream, the woods, the pond, and I mentally planned which I would visit first in my efforts to find her.

By 6am it was light enough for us to see and I hurried downstairs to find my parents still dressed and putting on their boots by the back door. I tugged on my boots and grabbed my coat and scarf from the hanger before following them outside into the chill morning air. A stiff breeze was blowing through the farmyard, kicking up leaves, dust and hay and blowing them here and there. I pulled my coat close around me as we huddled together to plan our search.

'We'll split up,' my father said. 'Isabella, you go with your mother. Where do you want to start searching?'

'The stream,' I said emphatically.

'Alright,' he replied. 'I'll head to the old barn across the way; maybe she went there to take shelter.'

We parted ways, my father heading off north while my mother and I headed south towards the stream. My instincts told me that Bessie would head towards water and the stream was closest, but she could have wandered for miles during the night. My mother seemed to sense my rising anxiety for she said:

'Don't worry, Isabella. She'll be alright – trust me.'

The wind was behind us, buffeting us on towards the stream as though helping us on our way. When we arrived there at last, we separated briefly to search up and down the banks, but there was no sign of her. I looked everywhere for hoof prints, but it was clear she had not been here. I suggested we try the woods next and so we set off across the fields, but this time

I scoured every inch of ground around us for the tell-tale hoof prints that would lead us to her.

We reached the woods soon after and the sight of them filled me with a mixture of fear and excitement. I had always been scared of these woods. For some reason no light seemed able to penetrate the foliage and so peering between the trees was like looking into a pitch-black void. I had been in there many times with my friends and the thought of it still gives me a thrill.

I doubted that Bessie would have gone in there, but I wanted to leave no stone unturned. I grasped my mother's hand and together we walked into the shadow of the leafy canopy. As we searched we called out Bessie's name in the hope that she would be drawn to us, but after half an hour in the dark and silent woodland we had to admit that she was not there.

After losing our way several times we finally exited the woods and headed towards the last place Bessie was likely to have gone to: the pond.

The pond was a popular picnic destination during the summer. It was situated at the top of a hill that overlooked the whole town and the countryside beyond. Ducks and other waterfowl frequented the area and a stand of trees on the east bank offered ample shade during the hot weather. At that moment the pond looked cold and steely, the surface almost mirror-like.

Standing on the west bank we could see no sign of Bessie and I began to lose all hope of ever finding her. With a sinking feeling in the pit of my stomach I began to move along the bank. As I walked I glanced down and spotted something in the mud, a hoof print. Bessie had been here!

I yelled to my mother to follow me as I began to hurry along the trail. It led south along the bank and up a steep rise, but when I crested the rise I found that the trail had ended abruptly. Where could she have gone? I spun full circle as I scanned the area for any sign of her. Nothing. I looked down at the ground once more and noticed deep scuff marks in the mud.

I tracked these marks with my eyes and finally spotted her. Bessie! She was lying prone in a dried-up streambed at the bottom of the rise and for a brief, horrible moment I thought she was dead. But at the sound of my anguished gasp she flicked an ear and raised her head off the ground. A wave of relief washed over me.

As I scrambled down the rise I realised that Bessie must have lost her footing and fallen down there during the night. How long had she lain there, hurt and alone? It brings tears to my eyes just thinking about it. My mother finally caught up with me and assessed the situation in an instant.

'Stay there,' she said. 'I'll go get help. Try and keep her calm and dress that wound if you can.'

I had not noticed any wound, but once I did I took action immediately. I took off my scarf and tightly bound the deep cut on Bessie's left foreleg.

She whinnied in pain but I stroked her nose to soothe her.

It was over an hour before my mother returned, but when she did, she did so with a veritable army of people behind her. My father and several other burly men took charge and coaxed Bessie onto the back of a special cart. Before long she was back in the stable being looked at by the best veterinarian in town.

It was such an eventful day that I did not have time to write about it until now. When I got home yesterday I flopped onto my bed and did not wake until late this morning! I hope my account of what happened has been of some interest. I need to practice my story writing skills somewhere if one day the whole world is to read my work!

July 26th 1942

I have just heard a very disturbing report on the wireless. I was heading to the kitchen to get a glass of milk when I heard my father listening to something in his study. He was so deeply engrossed in the report that he did not hear me approach, and so I stood silently behind him and listened.

I did not fully understand what it all meant, but it sounded to me like the Altegan nation is accusing the Kemalan nation of some crime or other, but the Kemalans are refusing to accept any responsibility for the alleged crime, instead making claims of their own that the Altegans contravened some agreement they shared. The report – or at least my understanding of it – was vague at best, but the last thing I heard was the newsreader warning of dire repercussions in the next few days.

My father realised I was standing behind him and shut off the wireless before I could glean any more information, then sent me away at once, but not fast enough for me to avoid seeing the worried expression on his face…

July 27th 1942

The newsreader was right. My father just returned from his usual delivery and I could tell at once that something was wrong. My mother and I were sitting in the kitchen when he arrived. Although we greeted him enthusiastically, he did not say anything. Instead he laid a newspaper on the table and stepped back for us to read it.

The headline blared at us across time and space, a herald of our futures:

WAR DECLARED!

I did not need to read any further. The expression on my father's face said it all. I don't much feel like writing any more just now…

CHAPTER 4
My First Escape

With Isabella's words still swimming before my eyes, I looked up dazedly from the diary to find someone tapping me on the shoulder. The tapping was insistent, anxious, and I looked down the length of the arm to see who it was.

An old man, bent with age, withdrew his hand and nodded at the diary before pointing towards a soldier striding towards us.

'I'd put that away if I was you,' he said. 'If they see it they will take it from you.' I nodded my thanks to the man and hid the diary in my coat, just as the soldier passed by us. His gaze swept every man, woman and child in the area, searching for any signs of trouble.

I kept my head down and hunched my shoulders, trying to remain as inconspicuous as possible. If my planned escape was to go off without a hitch, the best thing I could do was to try to remain invisible so my absence would not be noticed. Once the soldier had passed by I was able to raise my head once more and get the lie of the land.

I had been so absorbed in Isabella's world that I had almost forgotten where I was. I felt as though I had awoken from a long sleep and the stories I had just read were a dream. Isabella's life reminded me so much of my own, from the similarities between our parents, to the description of her home town, to the way her father had laid the paper on the table when the war was officially declared. I felt a connection to her that I could not explain, and it only heightened my resolve to complete the task I had set myself.

I realised then that I had been neglecting Ada. I looked down at her guiltily and stroked the soft hair on her head. She nuzzled my hand and licked my palm affectionately and I could not stop a smile spreading across my face. Whatever else happened I still had a friend in this world, and that was a comforting thought indeed.

The sun was sinking behind the distant mountains and the road around us was gradually growing darker. In the gathering gloom, several of my fellow prisoners stumbled upon rocks and potholes and one old lady tripped and fell, hurting her wrist. I spotted a couple of the soldiers talking quietly together and I could only assume they were discussing when and where we should stop for the night.

My assumption proved correct, for not long after this we were led off the road through a broken gate and into a field bordered by a low stone wall with trees on one side. I looked up at them as we passed. Against the darkening sky they looked like charcoal drawings, mere skeletal outlines, their branches creaking and groaning under a heavy north wind.

Why they had chosen to stop here, I did not know. From my point of view it seemed very exposed; there was no shelter from the elements and most importantly, and worryingly, there was nowhere to hide…

However, I was not discouraged. There was nowhere to hide, but soon the darkness would be my cloak. If I could leave the group without anyone noticing me, it was unlikely they would spot me before I made it across the field. I just had to be patient and pick my moment.

We were led into the centre of the field and shepherded into a rough circle. At first, everyone just stood there, milling around, fear and uncertainty etched into every face, then one of the soldiers took command and barked at us to 'Sit!' like we were dogs. And like good dogs we heeded the command and sat at once, heads bowed in a subservient way that made my blood boil. No man should be treated like this; like an animal.

I sat there, quiet and still, my furious gaze locked on the soldiers standing on the outskirts of the group and I stroked Ada's warm body to try to calm myself. Anger was beginning to override fear and it was clouding my judgement. I needed to remain clear-headed and focussed if I was going to escape unnoticed.

To distract myself from my anger I looked up into the sky and observed a pair of bats flitting overhead, struggling valiantly against a strong wind that sought to blow them off course. As I watched, I saw in them a parallel of my own life; indeed, of the lives of every man, woman and child on this planet.

In life it seems that we are always battling against a current. In most instances we know where we want to be, yet certain aspects beyond our control – be they time, nature or indeed other people – seem to want to keep us from reaching our destination. This situation is worsened in cases where we do not know our destination, when we are lost and unsure; the current takes hold stronger than ever and pushes us here and there on a whim, callously playing with us.

But it is this same current that gives us purpose. Without resistance, without an opposing force, we would simply glide through life and nothing we did would carry any weight, nor sense of achievement. It is in overcoming this current, in defeating its attempts to control us, that we achieve true satisfaction.

I smiled as the bats finally made it across the field and disappeared from view, and felt a new vigour for my cause engulf me. No one said this was going to be easy, but then nothing this important is ever easy, and I knew the journey I was embarking on was of the utmost importance. But at the time I just did not know why.

The soldiers had stopped talking and were now splitting up. Two of them had clearly drawn the short straws for they had been assigned to guard our group. One of them came and stood quite close to me while the other moved to the opposite edge and sat down upon a hillock. I cursed quietly under my breath. Under the watchful eyes of the guard this was going to be a lot more difficult than I had imagined.

I looked over to where the remaining soldiers had retreated and saw sparks suddenly flare in the darkness. The sparks landed on some hastily gathered wood and tinder and soon a flickering blaze illuminated the corner of the field, silhouetting the soldiers who sat around it warming their hands.

I noticed the guard standing close to me look longingly towards the fire, then sit down morosely upon a rock and rest his arms upon his rifle. Judging by the weary slump of his shoulders, I knew I would not have long to wait before putting my plan into action.

Several minutes had passed and the guard's eyelids had started to droop. I was just about to begin moving towards the edge of the group when I heard footsteps approaching and froze at once. Three of the soldiers had come bearing food and they ordered the guard to distribute it among the prisoners. They were so close I could smell the smoke on their clothes.

They turned and left and as they retreated back to their warm fire I heard the guard muttering irritably as he passed the day-old loaves of bread and flasks of water into the group. Then, in a much louder voice, he addressed us:

'Share it out evenly,' he shouted, barely hiding his obvious annoyance, 'it's all you'll be getting 'til tomorrow.'

I took the granary loaf I was handed and, with difficulty, tore off a small chunk from one end before passing it on. I then tore this in two and gave half to Ada, which she wolfed down in the blink of an eye. I chewed mine more slowly, for I had no idea when I might eat again.

A flask of water was then passed to me and I took a sip before pouring a small amount into my hand for Ada to lap up. I then passed on the flask and waited for things to settle down once more. It did not take long.

The food disappeared rapidly and rather than alleviating hunger, it intensified it. All around me I heard stomachs rumbling plaintively, like distant thunder. I too was still famished, yet I had no time to think about it. The guard's eyes were sliding closed once again and it was now full dark. This was the best chance I was going to get.

With my head held low I watched his face carefully, like a hawk surveying its prey. The time for action was near and as his chin flopped down onto his chest I made my move.

Carefully and quietly, I began to shuffle through the men and women seated all around me, with Ada following in my wake. Most of them had nodded off as fatigue got the better of them, so no one noticed my movements. Even so, I would stop every few paces and check that the guard was still snoozing before continuing on towards the edge of the group, to a point as far away from both guards as possible.

I was passing one of the prisoners – a woman I recognised – when she suddenly flailed her arms in her sleep and just missed hitting me. A low, anguished groan escaped her lips and her brow furrowed as she rolled onto her side and lay still once more. I wondered what nightmares had entered her head and I pitied her, for now both her dreams and her waking life were plagued with them.

I decided to take things more slowly. If she had hit me and awoken in shock, she might have given the game away. I changed course, opting for a longer route which would lead me through more open areas and lessen the chances of me knocking into anyone. My heart was racing as I inched my way along. It was like some horrible version of "What's the time, Mr Wolf?" Whenever I sensed movement close by I would halt immediately and sit down, so as to remain as inconspicuous as possible.

I was approaching the edge of the group and my pace was unconsciously increasing when, just at that moment, an owl hooted nearby. I stopped in my tracks – my muscles tensed, my breathing short and sharp – and turned my head slowly to check that the guard had not awoken. With a snort, the guard rubbed vaguely at his nose and then slumped further forward, his rifle slipping from his lap.

I breathed a sigh of relief and began to move on once again, edging my way cautiously past the last few sleeping prisoners. I stumbled over a submerged root and almost fell, but at last reached the edge of the group. We had made it, and all at once I felt incredibly exposed. The dark expanse of the field lay before me, its surface alive with shifting shadows. The wind whipped at my clothes as I crouched there, uncertain and terrified.

I could end this right now. I could sit back down and no one would be any the wiser. There was nothing forcing me to do this and, for all I knew, the owner of the diary could already be dead. I could just dump the diary and forget this ever happened.

Before I knew it the diary was in my hand, the muscles in my arm taut, like some part of me wanted to hurl it away. But I did not do it. Every rational, fearful bit of me screamed at me to stop this now, before it could begin. Images – triggered by fear – played out before my eyes, depicting my life on the run, and they petrified me. But still, I did not throw the diary away. I knew, somewhere deep beneath the tangle of fears and anxieties and cowardice, I knew that if I gave in this time, I would always give in – I would always live in fear. And I could not let that happen.

Giving it no further thought, I tucked the diary back inside my coat, took one final look around, then sprinted as fast and as quietly as I could north across the shadowy field to the dim outline of the wall in the distance. The wind roared in my ears as I ran and Ada, who was loping along at my side, found it difficult to maintain her direction. The low stone wall loomed suddenly in the darkness and I almost ran straight into it. I scrabbled at the stones as I hauled myself up and over, while Ada leaped gracefully to the top of the wall and hopped down the other side.

Now hidden, we crouched quietly together behind the wall, our chests heaving as we regained our breath. As we sat there in the stillness, obscured from view, I recalled a memory I had not thought of in a long time.

When I was much younger I used to play hide and seek with my father in our house and garden. We would take it in turns to hide and I both loved and hated this side of the game. There is an inherent thrill in hiding from someone; in knowing that you are being searched for and in exercising your cunning to choose a suitable hiding place. You feel your heart beat faster and faster as you watch your quarry hunt you.

But while I enjoyed this thrill on one hand, on the other it terrified me. The best hiding place I knew was a narrow alcove behind the shed in the garden and every time I went in there, I felt an unknown terror clawing at me and more often than not, I would sit there with my hands over my eyes, waiting for my father to give up and end the game, for he never once found me there.

I felt that same terror creeping over me now, only this time it was not unknown, and it was very, very real.

Taking a deep breath, I raised myself up and peeked back towards the group to see whether our escape had been noticed. It was difficult to see, but I discerned a vague figure walking towards the snoozing guard and my stomach turned over – it was the officer who led the squad. When he awoke the guard, would they notice I was gone?

The sound of his movements carried to me on the wind and I heard quite clearly the *thump* of the officer kicking the guard awake.

'Hey, you counting sheep?' he yelled at the guard. 'What the hell's the matter with you?' The guard snapped to attention at once and saluted his superior.

'I'm sorry, sir, I was just…' He began to say, then I watched, transfixed, as his eyes swept the group of prisoners. 'What the – where the hell is that boy? The one with the dog?'

'He's escaped?' the officer asked.

'I… I don't see him…'

'One of the prisoners has escaped!' the officer yelled so his men could hear. 'Spread out and find him, I want this boy captured alive!'

The sound of the officer's voice roused many of my fellow villagers and their confused and fearful murmurings were discernible even from here. I watched as the officer leaned close to the guard and whispered something in his ear then turned and walked away, leaving the man tense and still.

It was now so dark I had to strain my eyes to see anything. I needed to know which direction the soldiers would start searching in so I would know which way to run. My question was answered almost immediately. Indistinct, shadowy figures suddenly materialised less than fifty feet from my position and I panicked.

As I pushed away from the crumbling wall to begin running, a stone dislodged and I could only watch paralysed at what happened next. It fell, striking another stone on the way down, the resulting sound as loud as a gunshot.

I did not stop. I did not turn. I knew they would be right behind me. I knew they would be hot on my tail. I simply put my head down and ran, as fast as I could, in whatever direction my legs would take me.

CHAPTER 5
The Forest

The breath was torn from my lungs as I sprinted blindly onwards. My feet pounded the uneven ground like pistons and I swung my arms with each step to gain momentum. I could feel the blood pounding in my temples and a growing tightness in my chest. I was much younger than my pursuers, but nowhere near as strong. This was a race I could not win.

They were shouting at me, yelling commands, but the sound of my own heartbeat was heavy in my ears and I could not discern what they said. As the chill wind whipped past me, tears were ripped from my eyes and slid down my cheeks. What a fool I was. What made me think I was capable of all this? What made me think I could escape these trained soldiers and embark on a mission that would make a grown man blanch? It seemed I had made a terrible mistake, and I would very quickly be shown the error of my ways.

I looked back to check on Ada and saw that she was following closely in my footsteps and showing no signs of tiring at all. In fact she looked as fit and as fresh as if she had just woken from a good nap. I turned back just in time to narrowly avoid hitting a signpost that was stuck haphazardly into the grass. It was still so dark that I was not able to read what was written on it before I was past it.

In the depths of my frightened and weary brain I thought how strange it was to have a signpost in the middle of a field, but I did not have the time or energy to dwell on this thought. I just had to keep on going.

In the distance I could see what appeared to be the outline of a forest. If I could make it there before they caught me, I might have a chance. My father had taken me hunting and tracking with him many times and I had picked up a few basic tricks.

I stumbled on a raised bump in the grass and as I pitched forward I noticed many such bumps dotted here and there all around me. I righted myself and continued running, but a cold realisation was spreading through me. As the realisation became a certainty I began to slow, but it was not quick enough.

I felt my left foot land on something buried in the ground which then depressed under my weight with a metallic *click*. I froze instantly, leaving my left foot exactly where it was.

Oh no.

Oh no, no, no.

I had run right into the middle of a minefield.

I tried to regulate my breathing, clear my head, think rationally and find a way out of this, but a soldier's voice cut through my thoughts.

'Kid! Don't move! You're in a minefield!' I recognised the voice. It was that soldier again; the one who had chased after me when I found Ada, the one who had brought me back to the group when I found the diary. I turned to look at him and I could just about make him out in the darkness. He had stopped just short of the signpost.

'We don't want you to get hurt,' he continued. 'Just come on back to us slowly and carefully.' The other soldiers had gathered behind him and they were conversing in low tones, but their voices carried to me even here.

'You two, circle round in case he tries to continue north,' one of them said. 'Whatever you do, don't lose him.' Two of the men saluted and split up, one heading east around the border of the minefield, the other west. My time was fast running out. I needed to get myself out of this situation before I was surrounded. Fortunately, I knew just what to do.

During my history lessons I had learned a lot about the first Grand War. We had studied all the major battles and military figures on both sides and had discovered as much about bravery as we had about atrocity. But at this moment one story of bravery and quick thinking stood out above all else.

A soldier by the name of Benjamin Marcus had taken it upon himself to lead a group of civilians out of a conflict zone to safety. Against the orders of his superior officer, he had left his post at nightfall and gathered up as many non-combatants as he could find. He had then led these people down an unguarded backstreet and out of the disputed area.

But whilst traversing a deserted dirt road, one of his group had stepped on a landmine. The poor man did not know what to do. If he moved his foot, the mine would surely explode, killing him instantly. For a moment, Benjamin was at a loss. He did not want to leave the man behind, but they did not have long to waste.

After carefully checking the area ahead, he moved the rest of the group further up the road before returning to the stranded man. Taking a large rock from a ditch close by, he got down on hands and knees and moved slowly towards the man's foot, which was pressed firmly upon the mine's trigger.

Benjamin moved the rock into place beside the man's foot and told him to *slowly* slide his foot out of the way. As the man did so, Benjamin slid the rock into place upon the trigger, and the man was able to run back to his family.

I looked down at my foot and knew that my only hope was to mimic Benjamin's quick thinking. If I could not find something to replace my weight on the trigger, I was finished. I turned to check on Ada and saw that she was sitting placidly behind me, her tail sweeping the grass. I signalled her to *stay*, and she lay down upon the ground.

I crouched down gingerly, making sure to keep as much of my weight as possible on the trigger. I then scoured the ground with my hands, feeling blindly for a rock or even a heavy clump of dirt. There was nothing in the area in front of me. I eased myself around so I was facing the other way and patted the ground, desperation beginning to set in.

My palm closed on a spur of stone sticking out of the ground and my heart leapt. I tugged at it but it did not budge. It was buried in the earth. I tried to remain calm as I scratched at the grass, clawing great chunks out and dropping them to one side.

I had to hurry.

Once I felt I had cleared enough earth away, I tugged at the stone again and this time it shifted, but it still did not come loose. I pulled harder, frantic tears rolling down my face. As I strained to pull it out, my left foot moved and I heard a click from the mine. I squeezed my eyes shut, fearing that this was the end… but nothing happened.

Breathlessly, I gave the stone one last mighty tug and it came free in my hands. Feeling unduly exultant – given what I was about to attempt – I placed the stone down and began to slide my left foot to one side whilst sliding the stone in after it. My heart was in my mouth as I made the last tiny movement of my foot, and the stone took the weight of the trigger.

I flexed my foot, which was now stiff and heavy, and checked all around me to see where the soldiers had got to. The two men flanking me had vanished. It was possible they had already got ahead of me and could even now be waiting for me to run into their waiting grasp. But I had no choice. The forest was my best bet and I had to head towards it.

I called Ada to heel and began to pick my way warily between the mines. I knew that every step I took could be my last and the only way I was able to continue was by putting it from my mind and pretending I was playing some sort of game.

The forest was getting closer every second and even in the limited visibility, I could see that the number of mine-shaped bumps was becoming fewer. At last they disappeared completely. I knew I was through the minefield and for the moment at least, there was no sign of the soldiers.

I rushed onwards, hardly daring to believe I had made it. The dark confines of the forest ahead seemed like the most welcome sight in the world. In there I could hide. In there I could lose them.

Then a shout went up behind me.

'There he is! There he is! I see him!'

I had been spotted.

They could not have been more than one hundred yards behind me. My legs felt like they were made of stone, but I forced my flagging limbs forward and finally made the tree line. With Ada at my heels I dashed between the trees, knowing that I could not go on like this much longer. Thankfully I did not have to. I had a plan.

On one of my many hunting trips with my father he had taught me about tracking and trails and how to avoid detection, an inherent part of being a good hunter. It may seem strange that a coward like me would enjoy hunting, but it was not the hunting I enjoyed so much; rather the time I got to spend with my father. And I think that my father enjoyed it too, for on these all-too-brief trips I was to him a normal son, and not just an innate coward. That is not to say my father disliked me for my cowardice, but during these trips I was somehow able to forget my anxious nature and act more like a man.

Thanks to my father I knew how to throw these soldiers off my scent, but before I could do that, I had to hide Ada. As I ran I cast around for a hiding place and luckily spotted a hollow tree trunk lying in a clearing. It was too small for me to hide in, but it was just the right size for Ada. I pointed at the tree trunk and beckoned her inside and she enthusiastically obliged.

'Stay here, I'll come back for you, I promise,' I whispered. I then marked the spot in my mind and hurried deeper into the forest.

Once I had run an adequate distance I stopped and retraced my steps, taking care to step in my own footprints so as to create a false trail. I could hear their voices more clearly now and I knew I had little time. With the last of my strength I hauled myself up into the branches of a gnarled old oak tree and climbed as high as I could.

When I could climb no higher I stopped and slumped into the fork between two branches, then stared down at the forest floor far below. My limbs were shaking with fatigue and fear and I had to grab my wrist to stop it juddering against the branch. I had hidden myself just in time, for below me a twig snapped loudly and a soldier hurried into view.

Wide-eyed, I watched as he cast around for me and spotted my footprints in the soil. He yelled to his comrades and soon three more soldiers appeared below my tree and ran off down the trail I had laid. An eerie silence fell over the forest. There was not a sound to be heard anywhere; no animals, no birds, nothing.

Had my ruse worked? When the trail ended, would they give up the hunt and leave? I had no idea, nor did I know how long I would have to stay in this tree before it was safe to climb down. I just hoped against hope that Ada would stay where I left her. If they found her, heaven knows what they would do to her. They might use her to lure me out by threatening to hurt her, and I would not let that happen.

'Please stay where you are, Ada,' I whispered. 'Please stay there.'

With nothing else to do, I tried to make myself as comfortable as possible in the tree. I lay on my back and looked up into the pitch-black canopy above me. Through the tangle of leaves I could see tiny slivers of the night sky and several beautiful stars gleamed in the darkness.

'I wish I was home,' I murmured. 'I wish I was home...'

I must have fallen asleep, for I was startled by a sound close by. I rolled over to see the soldiers walking back along the trail below my tree. It was starting to get light and I began to worry that if they looked upwards they would see me.

'We've been searching all night,' one of them said. 'He's long gone. Let's just give up and head back.'

'Easy for you to say,' another hissed at him. 'You didn't lose the boy.' I recognised this man as the sleeping guard I had snuck past to escape.

'Well, do you want to keep searching?' the first man asked wearily.

'Frankly, I couldn't give a damn,' the guard replied, waving his machine gun in his agitation. 'He's just a young boy; if it hadn't've been me who lost him, I would have given up hours ago. But as it is...' He roared in anger, more at himself than anything else. 'The Captain is going to tear me a new one!'

In his anger he fired off a couple of shots directly upwards and one of the bullets grazed my shoulder as it passed. I bit my lip in shock and clamped a hand over the wound, but already I felt warm blood welling up beneath my fingers.

'Feel better now?' the first man asked condescendingly.

'A little,' the guard replied. The blood was now spilling over my fingers. If a single drop fell and they spotted it...

'Come on, let's get out of here,' the guard said resignedly. 'I'll take whatever punishment the Captain wants to dish out.'

They had just moved out from beneath me when a drop of blood fell from my fingers and landed on the leaves below. They were gone. I was safe.

I tried to sit up, but by this point I was so tired and in so much pain that I could barely move a muscle.

Just don't fall asleep, I told myself. My father had always told me on our hunting trips: *Never fall asleep when ill or wounded. Always do whatever you can to treat yourself before considering sleep.* I had to get up. I had to bandage this wound. But I was so tired. My eyelids fluttered closed.

I just need to rest my eyes, I thought. *Just don't... just don't fall...*

CHAPTER 6
The Parachute

The sun's rays on my face brought me back from my fevered dreams. My eyes cracked open and I peered up through the high tree canopy at the spots of brilliant light punching through the leaves. I tried to sit up and almost fell. With a jolt, I realised that I was still in the tree. At the same time I felt a dull, throbbing pain in my shoulder and remembered the wound I had sustained the previous night.

Stupid, stupid!

I had done precisely what my father had warned me never to do. If I did not act quickly I would be overcome by fever and out here – in the middle of nowhere – I would die.

I checked the wound and saw that the flesh around the cut had turned an angry red and pus was beginning to gather. Carefully, so as not to open the wound any further, I tore two strips from my shirt and cleaned the wound with one before using the other to bind it, using my teeth to tie the knots. It was not a good job, but in the absence of anyone to help me, it would have to do.

Feeling decidedly light-headed, I clambered down the tree and got my feet back on solid earth. It was just in time, for a wave of nausea washed over me and I was forced to throw out a hand to steady myself against the tree. When it had passed I looked around, trying to remember where I had left Ada. I knew I had hidden her in a hollow log, but I could not for the life of me remember where. The events of the previous night were fuzzy.

I was sure the soldiers were long gone by now, so I put my fingers to my lips and let out a piercing whistle I hoped Ada would hear. But she did not come running and there was no answering bark; the only sound I heard was a wood pigeon welcoming the new day.

I put my fingers to my lips once more and my whistle rang out long and loud between the trees. I waited, stock still, listening intently. Then I heard her. Her joyous voice echoed through the stillness as she barked a greeting and came loping into view. I got down onto my knees as she ran towards me and I hugged her tight, burying my face in her scruff.

'I'm sorry I left you alone,' I whispered. 'I'm sorry...'

She looked at me; tongue lolling, eyes bright, and I knew that she felt no ill will towards me. She was forever trusting, and forever faithful.

Stroking her absentmindedly, I glanced around us as I tried to get my bearings. I had become so turned around during our headlong flight the previous night that I was no longer sure which direction we should walk.

'This way's as good as any,' I said to Ada, pointing directly ahead of us down a rough path. We set off together, with me unsteady on my feet and Ada as sure-footed as a mountain goat. My wound shifted with each step we took and I was forced to keep my hand pressed against it to prevent it opening any further. I gritted my teeth and tried to focus on the task at hand: *Get out of this forest and find the means to fix myself.*

It would be easier said than done.

We had been walking for about half an hour and the forest was showing no signs of ending. I was beginning to get seriously worried. I knew the fever was starting to take hold for I was feeling alternately hot and cold and I was shivering uncontrollably. Ada seemed to sense that something was wrong and she was licking my hand sympathetically as we walked.

A strange shape materialised in the distance and I stopped to try and discern what it was. From this distance it looked like a low hill between the trees, but something about it was off. As we drew nearer I saw the sharp, broken lines of the object and knew that this was no natural occurrence. As we drew closer still the markings on the object became clear and I realised what it was.

It was the broken and twisted remains of a fighter plane.

The machine's chassis was badly charred and debris lay all around it in a wide circle like fallen snow. I signalled to Ada to stay where she was. Broken glass and shredded metal crunched under foot as I stepped cautiously near. A blade from the propeller was buried in a tree trunk close by and I ducked underneath it as I moved towards the cockpit.

I don't know what I was expecting to find there. It was clear that no one could possibly have survived this. When I drew level with the plane I discovered that it was empty. There were no bodies to be seen but on the inside of the glass I noticed what looked like spots of blood.

I climbed up onto the broken wing to get a closer look and it creaked ominously beneath me. Not wanting to actually climb inside, I got down onto my knees and stuck my head into the cockpit. The electrics were shot and blackened by fire and shards of glass lay everywhere. The pilot's seat had vanished and I realised that he must have ejected before the crash.

I knew what I was looking for but I did not spot it; if the pilot had ejected, he would likely have taken his first aid kit with him. Feeling downhearted, I turned my head to inspect the instruments more closely and noticed something stuck above the altimeter. It was a photograph. I reached towards it and lifted it clear and as I did so, half of it crumbled to ash.

I stared at what remained of it and saw a stunningly beautiful woman grinning shyly at the camera. Her hands were clasped at her breast and an arm rested lovingly around her shoulders. The owner of which was now obscured by fire damage, but I knew at once that it must be the pilot. In the background was a picturesque little cottage, behind which the sun could just be seen poking out above a stand of trees. For several moments I could not tear my eyes away from that photo.

It brought home a realisation that had never occurred to me until now. All this time I had been seeing these soldiers through a veil of hate. To me they were merely faceless oppressors; it had never crossed my mind to think of them as human beings. Human beings with families and ambitions; people both loved and loving. The juxtaposition was almost too strong for me to comprehend – here in this picture a loving husband, while here before me, evidence that he was also an instrument of war.

I reeled at the thought of it. I was too young and inexperienced to understand what I was seeing. The only thing I could think was that I did not know the man. I did not know what drove him down this path, and until I did I could not condemn him. I took one last long look at the photograph then tucked it inside my coat.

As I climbed back down the wing I felt the whole chassis wobble beneath me. Metal squealed and shifted and loose debris clattered to the ground. I jumped clear and landed awkwardly, narrowly avoiding a piece of metal sticking out of the mud. The whole chassis crumpled in on itself and a plume of ash was kicked high into the air. The noise was deafening and it echoed off the surrounding trees.

As the sound faded it was replaced by another; a low, chilling, mournful call that at first I could not place. I was sure it was not coming from the wreckage of the plane and when I looked at Ada I saw that her hackles were up and she was growling deep in her throat.

'What's the matter Ada?' I asked her quietly. 'What have…' And then I saw what had spooked her.

They came slowly, stalking between the trees, not rushing at all, savouring my fear; their eyes alight with murderous intent. Their footfalls made no sound upon the forest floor as they prowled towards us. There were three of them and as they moved they fanned out to prevent our escape. I had never encountered them before, but I knew of their vicious reputation.

Wolves.

Their jaws were slick with saliva and the left-most one of the three had thrown back its head and was emitting that dreadful howl. When it lowered its muzzle and the howl stopped, it was almost worse. The absence of any sound as they advanced was terrifying.

I moved closer to Ada, too shocked and frightened to run, and looked all around us for a weapon. The only thing I could see was one of the broken propellers lying close to hand and I bent down to pick it up, not taking my eyes off the wolves. It was very heavy, but in the circumstances it seemed like that would work in my favour. It would not do to try and fight them off with a twig.

By this point they had formed a rough semi-circle around us and were gradually forcing our backs against the wreckage. There was nowhere to run and even if there was, I was too weak to get very far. The fever was taking a stronger hold and I felt my head throb more painfully every second. Our only hope was to fight.

Ada's lips were drawn back over her teeth in a snarl and she looked ready to tear the wolves apart in a heartbeat. Every one of her muscles was tensed and ready, and when she made a movement towards them I stopped her.

'Steady,' I told her. 'Not yet.'

One of the wolves – bolder than the others – broke from the formation and padded closer, its eyes fixed on me, ignoring Ada completely. As it advanced I continued my cautious retreat until my heel came back in contact with the plane's broken wing.

The wolf took a few steps nearer and Ada decided that was quite close enough. With a fierce bark, she launched herself at it and knocked it to the ground, tearing at its throat with her sharp teeth. The two remaining wolves were taken aback at the ferocity of the attack, but they recovered quickly.

One of the wolves hurried to aid its stricken fellow while the other sprinted towards me. Out of the corner of my eye I saw Ada pause her frenzied attack and for a second she watched as the wolf ran at me, but she could not disengage herself from the struggle in time to help.

I hefted the broken propeller in both hands and felt my arms tremble under its weight. The wolf leapt at me, aiming for my throat. I swung the propeller and connected sharply with its shoulder, the impact reverberating throughout my whole body. With a yelp the wolf tumbled to the floor amidst the wreckage.

The force of my swing almost carried me to the ground as well, but I kept my footing and shakily raised the propeller again. The wolf got unsteadily to its feet and turned to face me, its eyes blazing hate. This time it came at me more slowly; wary now. It crept towards me, forcing me to step back onto the wing.

I knew I did not have much fight left in me and the wolf seemed to sense that too. It was looking for an opening, and it was only a matter of time before it found one. Desperate and terrified, I swung at the wolf a couple of times but each one went wide. By now it had forced me right up against the cockpit. Without warning it feinted to my left and I swung for it, just as it ducked back to my right. The wolf had found its opening and it took it, lunging towards me and bulling into my chest.

All the wind was knocked out of me as I fell flat on my back on the wing and the wolf leapt on top of me. I held the propeller in both hands and used it to force the wolf's head back as it tried to bite at my throat, its jaws inches from my face. Its breath was hot and stank like nothing I had ever smelt before.

My strength was waning and the coward in me wanted nothing more than to give up. It would be so easy. If I gave up now I would not have to go through with this insane task I had set myself. I could give myself over to death and be reunited with my parents. And I wanted so badly to see them again…

I looked over at Ada and saw that she had dispatched one of her aggressors and was valiantly fighting the other, and I knew at once that she would never just give up. As much as I wanted to see them again, my parents would not want me to give up either.

Gathering the last of my strength, I kicked upwards into the wolf's belly and sent it soaring over my head. It fell towards the cockpit and, with a sickening noise, was impaled upon the broken glass of the windshield. The wolf gave a last, agonised whine, and was still.

The propeller fell from my limp grasp and my chest heaved with exertion as I lay my head down upon the wing. My eyes slid closed and I welcomed the darkness, but the sound of pounding footsteps made me look up and I saw that the remaining wolf was almost upon me. I tried to move, to get out of its path, but it was too late.

Then, from out of nowhere – or so it seemed – Ada appeared. She barged into the wolf and sent it crashing to the ground nearby, then stood over me protectively, her fur stained with blood. They squared off against each other, both snarling viciously, then the wolf looked at the bodies of its two comrades, and the growl subsided.

Resignedly, the wolf turned around and slunk away between the trees, disappearing into the distance. When Ada was sure it was gone, she moved towards me and licked my face until I sat up and acknowledged her.

'Thank you,' I said, touching my forehead against hers. 'Thank you.'

I had never before met a creature as loyal as Ada. She could have run away at any time and left me to my fate, but she didn't… and that is something about her I will never forget.

We left the wrecked plane behind and continued along our chosen path. I was in serious trouble now. The wound was beginning to turn black and I was seeing spots of colour before my eyes. For this reason I almost did not notice the figure ahead of us. When I did, I almost fell over in surprise.

I ducked behind a tree and peeked out to check whether I had been spotted, but the figure had not moved. It was staring straight at us, but there was something odd about it. From this distance it almost looked as if it was hovering just above the ground and while it stood straight, it was also slumped forward at the shoulders, as though dejected.

I moved stealthily closer, using the nearby trees as cover and keeping Ada firmly to heel. Something was sprouting from the back of the figure and I was not sure what it was. It was only when I came within ten paces of it that I realised it was suspended by ropes like some grisly puppet.

What on earth was going on?

I followed the ropes upwards and spotted a parachute caught high up in the tree canopy – and then it all clicked into place. This was the pilot of the crashed plane! He must have ejected just before impact and come to rest here.

I was not sure what to do and before I could stop myself, I spoke.

'Hello?' I said faintly. Then I cleared my throat and tried again, louder this time. 'Hello?'

The pilot did not respond. Throwing caution to the wind, I walked right up to him and peered into his face.

'Are you alright?' I asked, and as I got a better look at him, I recoiled in shock. The pilot's empty eyes stared at me out of a bloodstained face. He was dead, and by the look of him, he had been for some time. I could not be sure, but I believed that he was an Altegan. Feeling nauseated, but driven by desperation, I put a hand over my nose and mouth to mask the smell and began to search him. This was my last hope.

When I found nothing of interest in his pockets I reached for his pack and tugged it from his back. The body twisted and contorted – a macabre marionette – then the pack came free and I hurried to a safe distance.

I was by now on the verge of collapse and my fingers worked feverishly to undo the clasps and open the pack. I sagged with relief. The familiar symbol of a first aid kit greeted my bleary eyes. I opened it and dug around inside. Within it I found some clean bandages, a small bottle of antiseptic, some antibiotics and some painkillers.

Working quickly, I removed the bloody bandages, cleaned the wound and rebound it. A second search of the pack revealed a flask of water and I drank some to wash down the painkillers and the antibiotics. I was not sure how many to take so I just took two of each.

I also found a packet of hard-wearing biscuits so I ate a couple and gave another two to Ada, which she gobbled up gratefully. I could already feel my head beginning to clear and the throbbing of my wound was starting to lessen. After resting for around half an hour I felt able to stand up and decided it was time to move on.

I repacked the bag and slung it onto my back, then – repulsed and nervous as I was – I walked tentatively towards the pilot to perform one final search. In a holster at his hip I found a .45 semi-automatic pistol and in an ammo pouch I found a number of spare magazines. I packed these into my bag and tucked the pistol into my belt. My father had taught me how to use weapons during our hunting trips and, in times like these, it paid to be prepared.

I was about to walk away when something stopped me. I reached inside my coat and drew out the photograph of the pilot and his wife. I turned back to face the body and then, after a moment's hesitation, I slipped the photograph inside his jacket.

'I'm sorry,' I said, my voice barely audible. 'I'm sorry you never got to see her again.'

Then I turned and walked away with Ada trotting at my heel. We had a long way to go, but first things first – we had to find a way out of this forest…

CHAPTER 7
The Tank

We had been walking for several hours, taking the time to rest here and there, and at last it looked like we were nearing the edge of the forest. Not far ahead of us I could see a break in the trees and beyond that, what looked like a vast expanse of countryside. I had no idea if we were even walking in the right direction, but at that moment I found it hard to care. All I wanted was to be out of this damned forest and to see the sky again.

Even though I was still feeling shaky, I broke into a run and sprinted towards the forest fringe. Ada got caught up in the game and galloped alongside me, soon pulling out in front. I quickened my pace and brought myself level with her again, unable to keep a smile from my face. Side by side we ran, as though chased by demons, revelling in the feeling of being alive.

A cool breeze hit my face, spurring me on, and by some miracle I drew ahead of Ada and exited the tree line before her. I collapsed in a heap on the grass, gasping and laughing, and when Ada caught up she leapt on top of me and licked my face. I fended her off playfully then hugged her tight before sitting up and surveying the area around me.

As I looked across the empty fields my light-hearted mood was swiftly quelled and I stood up slowly to better see what was before me. A town – or at least what was left of it – stood in a shallow valley; its outline jagged and broken against the horizon. Even from here I could see the skeletal structures of the ruined buildings and I could not be sure, but it appeared to be deserted, the likelihood of any survivors slim.

War had visited this place too and my heart sank at the sight. Was nowhere going to escape unscathed from this terrible conflict? It made me wonder at the kind of people who made the decisions that caused all this. Were they unaware of the consequences of their choices, or did they simply not care?

Whatever the case, I decided it was time to plan my next move. I drew the diary from my coat and flicked towards the last entries, hoping to refresh my memory. Just as I recalled, it seemed that Isabella and her family had been taken west towards the Kemalan HQ in Scioli. I looked up towards the sun and noted that it was hanging low in the sky beyond the town. I was sure that by now it was late afternoon and that meant that west was straight ahead… and that put the destroyed town squarely between me and my destination.

I would have to go through it; there were no two ways about it. If I was to circle around, it would take far too long, and I was already very low on food and water. *And you never know,* I told myself, *there may in fact be survivors to help or provisions to be scavenged.*

I tucked the diary back into my coat, then opened my bag and swallowed another couple of painkillers and antibiotics with a gulp of water. Then I poured some water into my cupped hand for Ada to drink, repacked the bag and squared my shoulders. I stood stock still for a moment, not taking a step, and envisaged the journey ahead of me.

'I'm not afraid,' I told myself quietly. 'I'm not afraid.'

I took a deep breath and set off towards the town.

Entering the town was akin to walking into a cemetery. It was so quiet. The kind of quiet you desperately do not want to disturb; like being in a church or a library. You move slower, speak more quietly, even breathe differently so as not to disrupt the stillness, and more often than not, you feel as if you are being watched. In this case I knew, at least, that the dead were watching me.

There is nothing quite like being alone on a deserted street. The houses on either side of you could be full to the rafters with people, but standing there, with no one in sight, makes you feel like you are the only person left in the world. I knew I was not the only person left, but in that ghost town I could be forgiven for thinking so. My fears were beginning to get the better of me and so I kept Ada close by my side as we walked.

The town was a wreck – no-one could have survived this. Even if anyone had lived through the attack, I doubted they would have stayed amidst the crumbling remains. Nowhere was safe, and as if to prove my point, a roof beam collapsed in a building close by and I almost jumped out of my skin.

An uncanny urge to get off the main street crept over me and I ducked down an alley between two buildings. Ada's head was held low and her ears were swivelling this way and that. Could she hear something I couldn't?

The wall to my left had partially caved in and I could see the remnants of a once beautiful little kitchen. Against my better judgement, I climbed inside and moved towards the cupboards to search for food. I tried first one, then another, then another. Each was empty, devoid of anything at all, let alone food. Whoever had lived here must have cleared everything out. I prayed that it had been before the attack and not after. I jumped back down into the alley.

'No luck, Ada,' I said quietly. Ada cocked her head at this. 'We'll have to keep searching.'

Exiting the alley, I crossed the street and continued west through the town. The blasted remains of a hotel on my left caught my eye and I stopped in the middle of the road. The building was completely devastated. The entire front wall had been reduced to rubble and I could see into each and every one of the six floors. Bedrooms, bathrooms, hallways and dining areas stood exposed to the world like a child's dollhouse. The scale of the destruction was mind-boggling.

On the ground floor I could see into a dining area and beyond that I saw what appeared to be a kitchen. I decided that the possibility of finding food was worth the risk. The building was bordered by a chest-high wall, but I scaled this easily. It was only when I dropped down the other side that I spotted a gap in the wall to my right. I smiled in spite of myself.

As I moved into the shadow of the building, I surveyed the structure above me dubiously. The ceiling could collapse at any minute and put an end to my task in a heartbeat. An ornate chandelier shifted ominously and I skirted around it, heading through the dining area towards the kitchen. I was glancing nervously around as I tiptoed along when I spotted something lying beneath a fallen shelving unit. It was a person! Someone was trapped under there!

I hurried over and knelt down at the head of the unit, trying desperately to dig my nails underneath and get a good grip. Using all my strength, I heaved upwards and the shelf moved. I threw my full weight into it and managed to lift it up high and with the last of my strength I threw it to one side. It thudded to the ground and set the surrounding rubble trembling.

'It's alright,' I said, turning my attention to the survivor. 'You're going to be...' But I stopped when I saw the figure. It was a young woman; she couldn't have been much older than twenty five. She was dead. Her rib cage had been crushed by the weight of the shelf as it fell on top of her. Her sightless eyes looked right past me towards the pale blue sky and on her face was a look of innocent incomprehension.

I sank to my haunches and held my face in both hands. Tears welled up in my eyes at the injustice of it all. What had this woman done to deserve this? What possible purpose could her death have served? I moved towards her and lay my hand upon her forehead, then slid my palm over her face and shut her eyes forever.

I stood up and made my way to the kitchen, feeling numb and suddenly very, very tired. I searched through all the cupboards and found a few scraps of food here and there, which I packed into my bag. When I had performed a thorough search, I left the kitchen and returned to the dining room.

Ada was sniffing around beneath the chandelier when I detected a low but distinct tremor through the soles of my feet. With each passing second it became stronger until the ground beneath me was visibly shaking. The chandelier creaked and several bolts came loose and fell to the floor.

'Ada, move!' I yelled. 'Get out of the way!' She looked up and ran towards me just as the chandelier crashed down behind her. She yelped in surprise and turned to look at the tangle of metal that had almost killed her. I hugged her close, just to reassure myself that she wasn't hurt.

'Come on,' I said. 'Let's see what's going on.'

We left the hotel and moved deeper into the town, seeking to discover what was making the earth tremble. As we drew closer to the source I heard a noise – a deep, low rumble – and as it got louder I detected the mechanical whir behind the sound.

It was a tank!

My blood ran cold and without stopping to think, I crouched low, grabbed Ada by the scruff, and scuttled as fast as I could into the living room of the building directly ahead of me. I threw myself down behind a section of wall and peeked over the edge to get a good view of the street outside.

It was deserted. Perhaps the tank wouldn't come this way? I glanced around at the room I now found myself in and saw that both the south and east walls had been completely obliterated. This was not the best place to hide, I was far too exposed. I needed to find somewhere else, now!

I was about to stand up and make a break for the building opposite when the sound of the tank's engine suddenly doubled in intensity and it came into view around the edge of a damaged chemist's shop. The barrel of its cannon scythed across the street as it turned and headed towards my building.

I tried to control my breathing and remain focussed, but I was terrified and my teeth were chattering so hard it was making my head hurt. I forced myself to raise my head and take a look and I saw that the tank was now fully in view, flanked on both sides by armed soldiers. From my time spent as their prisoner I knew they were Kemalan, and it looked like they were patrolling the area.

I ducked my head as a soldier at the back of the group looked in my direction and I prayed he had not spotted me. As the tank drew level with my hiding place I shifted my weight, ready to run at a moment's notice. The soldiers were yelling to each other over the din. I could not hear much of what they were saying, but I discerned a few phrases like: '*All clear!*' and '*No sign of 'em!*' and '*Keep moving!*'

When I was sure the tank had passed me and moved off further down the street, I stood up slowly and made to climb through the shattered west window of the house, hoping to find a safer place to hide. However, as I put my weight on the window sill the crumbling brickwork supporting it gave way and collapsed. I tumbled to the floor, narrowly avoiding serious injury as the bricks crashed to the ground and shards of glass – dislodged from the window panes – lanced downwards.

I had hit my head in the fall and I raised it painfully to check whether anyone had heard the noise. Over a pile of debris I noticed the soldier – who had looked in my direction earlier – creeping cautiously towards my location, signalling to his comrades that he was going to check something out.

I panicked. I had to find a place to hide! The side door to the building opposite had fallen off its hinges and I darted inside. I found myself in a kitchen and looked around for a place to conceal myself, but none was immediately forthcoming.

In the centre of the room was a rug placed at a curious angle. I moved in to take a closer look and beneath it I noticed what looked like a crack in the floor. I lifted up the rug and slid it to one side. It was a trapdoor – it must lead down to a cellar! I found the handle and yanked it open, ushering Ada in ahead of me down the dark, uneven steps.

I climbed inside and attempted to close the trapdoor behind me, but try as I might, I could not shut it completely. It was jammed! There was nothing else for it. I closed it as much as I could, then hurried down the steps into the darkness.

It was pitch black down there and the air was chill and smelt of mould and damp. I headed towards the farthest corner and crouched down with my back to the wall. Ada was sniffing around in the corner beneath the stairs and I called her over. She came and sat down by my side, leaning amicably against me. She had no idea of the danger we were in.

In the distance I could still hear the rattle of the tank as it moved through the town, but besides that the only other sound was my own laboured breathing. Then a sound above me made me catch my breath and Ada's head swivelled towards the trap door. Someone was in the kitchen above.

He's going to see the trap door, I thought. *He can't possibly miss it.*

I reached behind my back and pulled out the pistol I had taken from the dead pilot and feverishly tried to remember what my father had taught me. I withdrew the magazine and checked it was full, then made sure the safety was off and chambered a round. My head snapped up at the sound of the trapdoor being wrenched open and almost at the same moment the tank opened fire with a thunderous *boom* – the town was under attack!

The soldier's feet came into view and he began to creep cautiously down the stairs, his weapon raised, sweeping the cellar. Behind him the trapdoor half closed with a bang and he spun back to face it, then returned to scanning the area with his rifle in its dim light. I raised my own weapon in turn and pointed it shakily towards him. If he came too close I would have to kill him, but if I fired a shot his comrades might hear. What was I to do?

He had reached the bottom of the stairs and was searching the corner Ada had been sniffing around. It was so dark in here that perhaps he would not see me and would leave of his own accord.

The tank's cannon boomed overhead once again and I gasped in surprise. The soldier's head whirled around and he began to advance towards me. The cannon fired again and again then went silent as he drew closer and closer.

My hands were trembling so much that the pistol was rattling and I was sure he would use the sound to locate me. I used my other hand to steady the weapon and levelled it at the soldier's chest. I had to wait for the next shot from the tank. If I timed it right, no one would hear my weapon discharging.

He was very close now, so close that I could hear his breathing, but still the tank was quiet. He was almost on top of me when at last the tank fired, and so too did I. The bullet tore through the soldier's chest and he dropped to the floor like a stone as the sound of the cannon fire continued to echo all around us.

I slumped back against the wall, my body shaking with fear and grief, and the pistol slipped from my limp grasp. The enormity of what I had done would not hit me fully for some time, but even then I knew... I had just killed a man.

Fortunately, or perhaps unfortunately, I did not have long to contemplate this. Through a haze of tears I looked over at the corner beneath the stairs, the corner both Ada and the soldier had searched, and I noticed a door crack open. This door was almost invisible to the naked eye, but now it was partly open I could discern its outline.

From the darkness within the hidden room a small figure crawled out and began to make its way tentatively towards me...

CHAPTER 8
The Survivor

I could not stem the flow of tears falling from my eyes so I dashed them away with my sleeve as I raised the pistol once more and aimed it at the figure that was walking hesitantly in my direction.

'Stop,' I commanded. 'Don't come any closer!'

The figure raised its hands – to show it was unarmed – but continued to move towards me, stepping carefully around the body of the dead soldier.

'I said stop!' I fairly yelled. 'I have a weapon… I…'

But the figure had stopped moving and sat cross-legged a few paces in front of me. I lowered the pistol suspiciously, still ready to use it at a moment's notice.

'Who are you?' I asked. At first it seemed that the figure was not going to answer. It looked down at its feet and fiddled with its shoelaces. Then it sighed and shrugged its shoulders and said simply:

'This is my home.'

I was stunned. I had come to believe there were no survivors of the terrible battles that had taken place here.

'You… you live here?' I asked.

'Well, not in the cellar,' it replied sardonically. 'At least, not until recently.'

'What's your name?' I asked.

'Hang on,' the figure said. 'I'll be right back.' It hurried towards the hidden room under the stairs and returned a minute later carrying something in each hand. It set one of the objects down, then I heard the unmistakeable sound of a match being struck. The match caught and a warm orange glow filled our corner of the cellar. The figure used the match to light a gas lantern it had brought, then set it between us and I was at last able to get a good look.

A scrawny boy of about eleven was revealed in the flickering light, his mop of hair wildly unmanaged and resembling a tangled hedge. His skin was pale, as though he had not seen the sun in some time, but his eyes were alight with the unmistakeable spark of youth.

'Marco Martolli,' the boy said, presenting a hand for me to shake. 'And you are?' I was so taken aback at this that I almost did not know what to say. I set the pistol on the floor and accepted his hand, shaking it meekly.

'Will… er, William Belmont,' I replied.

'Nice dog,' Marco said appreciatively. 'I used to have one like her, what's her name?'

'It's er… Ada… her name's Ada.'

'Come here, girl,' Marco said, beckoning to Ada. Ever trusting, Ada bounded towards him and tried to lick his face as he stroked her. Marco giggled as she knocked him to the floor and licked his cheek. I was still a little shocked at the unexpected turn of events, but I had too many questions to just sit there silently.

'So… what are you doing here?' I blurted out. 'Why haven't you left? And where are your parents?'

'That's a lot of questions in one go,' Marco said, raising his eyebrows at me. 'I can answer them all, but it's quite a long story…' Somewhere in the town the tank fired another shot, leaving in its wake a ringing silence.

'I don't think we'll be going anywhere for a while,' I replied. 'Tell me what happened.'

'OK, well…' Marco began, shifting to a more comfortable position and continuing to stroke Ada absentmindedly. He looked perfectly at ease and this baffled me still further, given the ongoing sounds of conflict above. 'I've lived here with my parents all my life; never even left the town before, so when the war started nothing really changed for me. It hadn't reached here yet so, as far as I was concerned, it wasn't happening. My dad tried to keep it from me as much as he could, you see. He's the best – he wanted me to go on enjoying my life as much as possible and not let the war ruin it. So, when it did finally reach us it came as a bit of a shock, I can tell you! But I was never scared. My dad's more than a match for any of those soldiers. I bet he could take on ten of them on his own! So, one day we got word that the Kemar… the Kemal…'

'The Kemalans?' I prompted.

'Yeah, them…were patrolling our area and before we knew what was happening, the Altegers arrived and their first attack began. The Kemarls saw them off but the Altegers have been attacking over and over ever since. We had no opportunity to run so we've been riding out the attacks down here, but we started getting low on food. One day it went quiet and dad said he would go out and search for supplies and check if the coast was clear for us to escape, but I reckon he was going off to fight them! My mum didn't want him to go on his own – she thought it was too risky. I told her it was only risky for the soldiers that crossed his path, but she wouldn't listen. Dad tried to make her stay with me, but she said I would be perfectly safe in the hidden room and in the end, he let her go with him. They said they would be back in a few hours but that was, hmm, two… three days ago now? I've lost track of time down here. But I'm sure they'll be back soon, once my dad's finished giving them what for.'

I did not know what to say. For all his confidence and assurances, it seemed clear to me that Marco's parents had been killed in the crossfire or captured by the defending Kemalans – but his faith in his father was so all-consuming, it was blinding him to the truth. I did not think he would believe what I was about to tell him unless I gave him reason to do so. I cleared my throat.

'I… I had a similar experience myself,' I began falteringly. 'I'd never really gone far outside my village either, so when the war started, all that really changed was we listened to the wireless a lot more and went outside a little less. We heard things; terrible reports of what was going on elsewhere, but it didn't actually reach us for some time. When those two armies clashed in our village, we were completely unprepared for it. My... my parents and I hid in our cellar while the mortars fell and the next day there was only one army left in our village – the Kemalans. They gathered up the survivors and led them off west towards their HQ in Scioli. I managed to escape along the way, but the rest of them are still being held captive and are on their way to the prison camps.'

'That's awful,' Marco said, cutting across my train of thought. 'Couldn't you have helped them?'

'I... what? No... I wouldn't have stood a chance against them. What I'm trying to say, Marco... is that I think your parents may have been captured too...' Upon hearing this, Marco sat bolt upright and gave me a harsh stare.

'What?! That's ridiculous! My dad getting caught by a bunch of Kemarl soldiers?' He snorted with mirth at the mere thought of it. 'Don't be silly! And even if he was caught, he could escape in the blink of an eye. If you can do it, my dad can do it!'

His belief in his father was overpowering. I knew I would have to try a different tack if I was to get through to him.

'That may be true,' I replied. 'But your mother was with him too. Maybe your father could have escaped easily, but it might not have been so simple for two people to escape.' I noticed the subtle change in Marco's expression and I knew I was beginning to get through to him. He stopped stroking Ada and furrowed his brow, his confident expression momentarily morphing into one of anxiety.

'Do you... do you think that could have happened?' he asked, sounding unsure of himself for the first time. 'You think maybe they've caught my mum, and my dad can't try anything for fear of them hurting her?'

I didn't enjoy being the one to break the news to him, but if someone didn't get through to him then he may never leave this cellar again. He would obediently stay hidden down here for the rest of his life, confident in the knowledge that his parents would return to him one day.

'That would be my guess,' I replied, nodding emphatically. At this, Marco leapt up and cracked his knuckles theatrically, flexing his neck as though he was about to go into the ring with a world champion boxer.

'Then what are we waiting for!' he cried. 'We need to get out of here and go help my dad, right now! He told me to stay in the hidden room, but that was before he knew that mum would get caught. I've got to go find him!' With this, Marco turned and began to make his way towards the stairs. I stood up quickly and rushed over to block his path.

'Hold on, hold on,' I said. 'There're soldiers up there and anyway, we can't just go running off without a plan or provisions or...'

At that moment there was a *thud* overhead, followed by footsteps across the floorboards. For a second I was back in the cellar of my home with my parents huddled on either side of me, holding me tight. I choked back a cry as the memory faded and immediately blew out the gas lantern and began to usher Marco across the darkened cellar to the hidden room.

'We've got to hide,' I whispered. 'Ada, come!' Ada trotted towards me as I bundled Marco into the room and once he was inside, I waved her in ahead of me. I could hear muffled voices now, coming from the kitchen above us. At first it was unintelligible, then I caught some of what they were saying.

'...he's not among the dead or wounded. Search the area, we have to find...' I did not need to hear any more. I ducked inside the room and closed the door behind me, leaving a small gap so I could see what was going on.

Marco shuffled around so he could see me more clearly.

'Whose side are they on?' he asked.

'Does it matter?' I replied. 'They're probably Kemalan.'

He was about to say something else when a sound from above made him shut his mouth. Someone was opening the trapdoor. We held our breath and sat as still as possible. Through the gap in the door I saw light spill down the stairs, then a shadow cut across it.

The shadow grew larger as whoever it was began to descend the stairs into the cellar. We could hear the heavy tread of his boots right over our heads, but the sound ceased around half-way down. There was a *click*, and the beam of a flashlight cut through the darkness, scouring the area. My heart stopped. If he spotted the body, we were done for. The task I had set myself would go unfinished and we would be lucky if we weren't killed on the spot.

I prayed he would not be too thorough and as the beam swept around it narrowly avoided revealing the dead soldier's boots. A shout from above made the torch beam vanish and after a heated exchange the trapdoor slammed shut and the footsteps receded.

As one, we breathed a sigh of relief and I slumped back against the wall, feeling more drained than I had ever felt in my life.

'OK, they've gone,' Marco said, getting to his feet. 'Let's go find my dad!'

'Are you mad?!' I said, pressing him back down. 'They won't have gone far – we have to give them enough time to leave the town before we head out again.'

'If you say so,' Marco said casually. He picked up a crumpled ball of paper and threw it for Ada who began to bat it around playfully. 'Hey, you want something to eat?'

'Yeah,' I replied. 'I'm starved.'

It turned out that Marco had been left the last of his family's dwindling food supply, but together we managed to concoct an adequate repast of potted meat sandwiches and glasses of milk, which was only slightly sour. By the end of it I was feeling full and very sleepy. My eyes began to get heavy as I realised that I had not slept properly for days.

I lay down on an old blanket and Ada curled up beside me. I had only intended to rest my eyes for a moment – not wanting to appear rude – but before long I was fast asleep and for a few hours I was able to forget my troubles and escape into a land without war.

When I awoke I found Marco sleeping peacefully close by and Ada scratching at the door and whining. She was clearly not too happy about being cooped up for so long. I opened the door cautiously and checked all around before letting her out into the cellar. I listened carefully for any sounds from above, then I roused Marco and told him it was time we were moving on.

'About time,' Marco replied. 'I gave up waiting for you to wake up and fell asleep too!'

Before leaving we packed up the remainder of Marco's food and drink and stuffed a couple of blankets into my bag as well. I searched around for anything else that might be of use and remembered the pistol I had left on the floor. I walked over to it and picked it up, flicking the safety back on. Then I tucked it into the back of my trousers.

As I was turning to leave, my eyes fell on the body of the soldier I had killed. I walked towards him and knelt by his side. I felt as though I should say something, but I did not know what. The irreparable act I had committed had still not fully sunk in.

'Hurry up, Will,' Marco said agitatedly from the foot of the stairs. 'Let's go, let's go!'

I did not reply and I still could not think of anything to say to the man I had killed. So instead I simply knelt there for a minute with my eyes closed and contemplated what I had done. When I felt ready to leave I stood up, cast one final glance at the body to burn it into my mind, then moved to ascend the stairs out of the cellar.

When I reached the top of the stairs I opened the trapdoor carefully and scanned the area for any sign of a threat. When I saw none, I opened it fully and let Ada and Marco out. Keeping close together, we left the confines of the ruined kitchen and stepped out warily into the street.

'Which way do we go?' Marco asked. 'Which way will they have taken my parents?'

'West,' I replied, shading my eyes against the glare of the sun and staring in the direction we would soon be walking. 'The same way they took everyone else.'

CHAPTER 9
The Boatmen

To our great relief, the town appeared to be deserted – it seemed the Altegans had finally given up attacking the area and allowed the Kemalans to withdraw. However, there were visible signs of the recent conflict all around us. Fresh craters – the result of grenade and mortar fire – riddled the street, and the still-smoking husk of a tank rested at an obscure angle against a pile of rubble. Shell casings and empty magazines littered the ground and here and there we spotted dank pools of blood.

Marco, seemingly unaware that we were not yet out of danger, chatted incessantly about everything and nothing. Given our predicament and the potentially dire situation his parents were in, his cheery spirits and airy demeanour seemed strange and alien to me. How could he appear so carefree with everything that had happened to him?

I had never been much of a talker, and I was not even that good a listener, but I did my best to appear interested in everything he had to say. That is not to say that what he said was not interesting, just that at the time my thoughts were elsewhere. I was thinking about the diary and whether this sudden change of events would impact my plans. Now that Marco was along for the ride, I would have to do my best to help him without deviating too much from the course I had set myself.

I felt bound to him now, for it was I who led the soldiers to his hiding place and it was I who led him away from the safety of that same hiding place. It was on me now to look after him and help him return to his parents, if they were even still alive...

Taking care of someone was not something I had ever done before. I had taken care of my first dog, Milo – until he sadly passed away – and now I was taking care of Ada, but I had never before taken charge of another human being; never been somewhat responsible for their safety and wellbeing.

Marco was still talking and, try as I might, I could not tune him out any longer. From the little I had gleaned from half-listening to him, he seemed to be talking about his life before the war. But when I heard him say the word "coward" I instantly started listening more intently, only to discover that he was talking about an incident that had occurred in his home town several years ago.

'When they called me that I decided to show 'em,' he said, a pugnacious undercurrent detectable in every syllable. 'I only didn't want to 'cos I knew I had to get back in time for dinner, but I wasn't going to let them call me that. So I went with them into the tunnel. It was pitch black in there, I can tell you! We only got about halfway before they all got scared and turned back, but I carried on and went right through to the other side. When I didn't reappear, they waited at the entrance, shouting my name. I decided to give them a little scare, so I doubled back and came round the outside of the tunnel and just as they were venturing inside to find me, I jumped out at them! They almost leapt out of their skins and we all fell about laughing!'

I smiled in response but in my mind I was thinking, *even this young boy is braver than me. If I had been in that situation, I doubt I would have gone into the tunnel. I would have run away, as I always have done...*

'My friends and I had a lot of fun back before the war started,' Marco continued. 'But now I don't know where they are, or even if they're still alive...' For a moment I thought he might – for the first time – be on the verge of tears. But then he bounced back almost instantaneously.

'Ooh, did I tell you about the time I shot milk out of my nose?' he asked. I could not stifle a snort of laughter at this completely, insanely out-of-the-blue question and I spoke for the first time in at least half an hour.

'You did what?!' I asked incredulously.

'Yeah!' he replied. 'I was having milk and biscuits at my friend's house and he told me this great joke he'd just heard and I laughed so hard that milk came shooting out of my nose! Then he laughed so much that he fell off his chair!'

I couldn't help it. I laughed until tears rolled down my cheeks.

'What was the joke?' I asked when I had recovered sufficiently enough to talk. 'What was so funny that it made you shoot milk out of your nose?'

'Ok, listen to this,' he said. 'Why did the chicken cross the road?'

'I don't know,' I replied. 'Why did the chicken cross the road?' Marco was still giggling and he could barely get his words out.

'How… how should I know, ask him!' At this Marco gripped his sides and roared with laughter while I looked at him askance.

'That's awful!' I said, laughing harder than ever.

'I know,' Marco replied. 'But it made you laugh, didn't it?'

Without realising it, we had already left the outskirts of the town and were now heading westwards across the fields. As we walked, Marco kept up a barrage of stories and anecdotes and before long, he had broken down my walls of solitude with his inimitable charm.

We ate up the miles as we chatted about books and sports, families and friends, loves and hates, and soon I felt like I had known him my whole life. In many respects I envied him. He possessed certain characteristics I could only hope to ever know. He was one of those people who seemed able to just talk and talk – but not in a bad way. He could start a conversation from nothing and set me off laughing in no time.

I had never been able to do that. I was always awkward around new people until enough time had passed that I was able to gauge what they were like and how to speak to them. My silence around strangers – in reality a crippling shyness – most likely came off as aloofness, or even disdain.

Marco, however, did not suffer from this affliction. I was perfectly sure that if he wanted to, he could walk up to any random person on the street and strike up an amiable and involved conversation, when I would be made nervous by someone stopping to ask me the time of day.

This was something I had always wanted to change about myself, but the more I thought about it, the more I realised that it was a gift, and it was a gift that had not been bestowed upon me. This was not something I could fix overnight. By deciding I wanted to change, I would not just wake up one morning, go out into the street and start chatting to anyone who would stop and listen. No, this gift was something that would take a while to earn, but in this swift friendship I had struck up with Marco, I believed I had taken my first step towards this goal.

The sun was riding high in the sky and with no shade close by, we were soon very hot and extremely thirsty. Ada's tongue was lolling and she was panting heavily, so we decided to take a quick rest and have a drink and a bite to eat. We threw together a couple of corned beef sandwiches and fed the rest of the corned beef to Ada, then drank our fill from the flask of water I had taken from Marco's hiding place.

Suitably refreshed, we set off once more and it was not long before I spotted something stuck into the ground on the crest of a low rise ahead. Marco noticed it too and as he did his pace gradually decreased until he stopped completely and stared uneasily in its direction. This was the first time I had seen any real display of anxiety from Marco, and so I was instantly on the alert.

'What is it?' I asked. 'What is that thing?'

'I think…' he began, struggling to go on. 'I think it's the forbidden zone…'

'The what?' I asked in bewilderment. 'Why is it forbidden?' But Marco did not seem to have heard me. He was looking past me, taking tentative steps backward, so I walked up to him and gripped his arm to stop his retreat.

'What does that thing mean?' I asked, pointing at the object stuck into the ground. Marco looked at me but he did not seem to see me. His expression was glazed, his eyes unfocussed. When he spoke he sounded like a different person.

'That's… that's where they dropped the bomb,' he said, in a voice that was barely audible. 'The atom bomb that ended the first Grand War.' I released his arm at once and stepped away from him, my eyes flicking to the object with a newfound respect.

'You're serious?' I asked stupidly, the answer already patently obvious. 'So that means..?'

'Yeah,' Marco replied. 'The whole... the whole area past that point has been irradiated for years... so my dad says anyway. He always told me never to go near it...'

I stared at the object as my history lessons came flooding back once more. I saw the events I had committed to memory playing out before me like a vivid daydream.

'So that's where their advance was halted,' I said, more to myself than to Marco, 'that's where the most evil nation on earth was stopped in its tracks. I've read so much about this place... I never thought I'd see it.'

I began to walk towards the low rise, wanting to take a closer look. Marco started after me, but then thought better of it.

'Where are you going?' he called anxiously. 'You shouldn't go near it... you shouldn't...' But when I didn't stop, he shook his head resignedly and followed cautiously in my wake.

I had almost reached the base of the hill when Marco caught up with me and tried to pull me back.

'It's dangerous,' he said. 'It might still be radioactive.'

'It's been over forty years,' I replied. 'The levels of radiation will be almost nothing by now.'

'You don't know that,' he said, tugging at my arm. 'Let's just go around it.'

'I only want a quick look,' I answered, jerking my arm free and hurrying ahead.

I began to clamber up the hill, stumbling now and then and falling onto all fours, and at last reached the crest of the rise. The object I had spotted earlier turned out to be a signpost upon which was the universal symbol for radiation and the words:

DANGER
RADIOACTIVE AREA AHEAD
DO NOT PASS THIS POINT

Raising my eyes from the sign, I looked out across the landscape before me and saw in the distance a sight that I had only ever seen in history books. It was a long way off, but the crater looked far wider than it ever had in those black and white images. The land around it was barren and empty, devoid of life or colour – a blasted wasteland where nothing would ever grow again.

The view made me sorrowful, but it also made me think. This was where tyranny was ended. Or perhaps I should say, this is where tyranny was put on hold. For with the removal of one tyrannical nation, two more sprang up in its stead, and that is how we found ourselves in this situation. Another war was now raging and neither side seemed ready to back down. Would this war end in the same way the last one had? Would another nation step in and end it for them? Would another atom bomb be used as a full stop on this war?

I did not have answers to any of these questions, but it was a terrifying thought – one that glued me to the spot and made me want to curl up and never move again.

Marco appeared at my side and tugged at my sleeve once again.

'OK, you've had a look – let's go, Will,' he said.

'Alright,' I replied, my eyes still fixed on the crater. 'Alright, I'm coming.'

Together we set off back down the hill and began to make our way around the northern perimeter of the forbidden zone. With the zone to our left we continued on westwards, but by this point it was beginning to get dark and black clouds were gathering overhead, threatening rain.

We needed to find a place to rest for the night, but nothing seemed to be forthcoming. In the gathering gloom we detected a strange sound ahead of us, like a strong wind, only louder, more intense. It was only when we were almost on top of it that we realised what it was.

It was a river. A wide, seemingly impassable river running north to south that blocked our path and roared in our ears. Against the fading light of the horizon I observed the silhouette of a forest to the south on its eastern bank. It was not far away and when I pointed it out to Marco he began to scurry towards it gladly, happy for anywhere that would shelter us from the inevitable rain. Thunder boomed overhead and the first spots of rain fell upon my face as I looked upwards at the turbulent sky. I drew my coat over my head, whistled at Ada to follow, and hurried after him.

By the time we entered the forest we were already soaked through and glad of the chance to rest. We decided to set up camp close to the tree line where we would have a good view of the surrounding countryside. This would allow us to keep an eye out for threats and plan our route for the next day.

I took off my sodden coat and hung it from a branch to dry, then sat myself down beside Marco and began to rummage in the bag for something to eat. Marco had not said anything since we had left the forbidden zone and I began to suspect that the sight had deeply affected him. It was clearly something that had scared him for many years – he must have heard stories about the lives that were lost that day and the effects of the radiation on the villages within the fallout zone.

I too had read many accounts of the innocent civilians who had died months or even years after the event due to radiation sickness, the symptoms of which are too ghastly to go into. It was a high cost to pay for an end to the war. I was glad it was not a decision I had had to make.

Marco was staring at Ada, his face immobile, and just when I began to think there was something seriously wrong with him, he turned to me and said:

'Can dogs think?'

I did a double take.

'What?' I asked, unsure whether or not I had just heard that.

'Can dogs think?' he repeated. 'Do you think she has ideas? Y'know – hopes, dreams, thoughts about us?' I smiled through my confusion, relieved that he was in fact the same old Marco.

'Er...' I began. 'I don't think they can form ideas exactly, but I'm sure they have some thoughts about people they meet. That's why they're excited to see their owners, but ferocious towards strangers.'

'Hmm…' Marco said pensively. 'When my dog was alive, I was positive he had hopes and dreams. I don't know what made me think that, I just always believed that was the case.' He grabbed a chunk of bread and began to munch on it.

'Hey,' he said, spraying crumbs everywhere. 'Did I tell you about the time me and my dog dug a tunnel under the house?'

For the next hour or so Marco talked and talked and at last fell asleep upon the bag with his mouth open, snoring gently. I chuckled to myself as I lay down to sleep and it was not long before I too was deep in slumber.

At around two in the morning I was awoken by a strange noise. Muffled voices were coming from the eastern bank of the river just north of our position and they were accompanied by the sound of something being dragged across the ground. I crept over to Marco and shook him awake, holding my finger to my lips so he would know not to speak.

Side by side, we tiptoed right up to the edge of the forest and lay down on our bellies, looking out at the river. It had turned into a beautiful night. The stars were out and the scene before us was lit by pale moonlight.

Several men dressed in plain clothing were hefting a heavy looking row boat towards the river. They were speaking in hushed tones and on more than on occasion they almost dropped their burden. They did not look like soldiers, but where on earth were they going at this time of night? What business did they have crossing the river at two in the morning?

I was just about to turn and ask Marco what he thought when I noticed something on the brow of the hill behind the boatmen. The moonlight was glinting off something metallic and it took me several moments to realise what they were.

Rifles.

There were soldiers hidden on that hilltop and it did not take a genius to figure out what they were planning. My eyes flicked back to the boatmen, who by now had waded into the water and were setting the boat down in the shallows. I looked back as the soldiers crawled into view and raised their rifles to firing positions.

I stood up and just as I screamed, 'Look out! Behind you!' the soldiers let rip. Muzzle flares lit up the area around them and gunshots echoed deafeningly across the countryside. I leapt to Marco's side and covered his eyes to protect him from the sight, but I could not protect myself. I stared, frozen, as innumerable bullets tore into the helpless men, dropping them where they stood in the muddy, swirling water.

Within seconds it was over. Dumbstruck, I shooed Marco away and he did not protest. I had fallen to my knees and I watched, horrified, as the soldiers descended from the hill and moved towards the bodies. Coldly, the soldiers searched the corpses, removing several small firearms. They spoke to each other and gesticulated, but I could not hear their words, then they walked away, leaving the men where they fell.

I walked back to our makeshift camp like someone in a dream. Had that really just happened? Had those men really just been murdered in cold blood? I sat down opposite Marco, too shocked and scared to speak. Marco was in a similar state. The combination of encountering the forbidden zone and witnessing those murders seemed to have finally shattered his outward show of bravery.

We sat there silently for over an hour before Marco could no longer keep his eyes open and fell asleep. But sleep would not come to me. Instinctively, I reached for the diary with shaking hands and flipped it open, seeking to calm my frayed nerves. I found the last entry I had read, and read on from there…

CHAPTER 10
Isabella's Story: Part 2

August 26th 1942

Picking up this pen again feels strange somehow, almost alien. It feels like an object from another life, the purpose or use of which now long forgotten. I look at it as someone might look on a childhood friend they haven't seen for many years. There are things you recognise, some familiarity, but you no longer quite know who this person is anymore.

As I sit here writing, I wonder at how something that was once so familiar could have become so different, so unknown, so "other". It has only been one month since I last wrote in this diary, yet it feels to me like a lifetime ago. As I flip back through past entries I almost do not recognise the author, for I find it hard to identify the cheerful, carefree girl of these anecdotes as myself.

Much has changed in the intervening month, but in truth, that in no way does it justice. Our lives have been turned upside down and I have been introduced to a world that I could not have imagined in my worst nightmares. And it all happened so quickly. Mere days after reading "WAR DECLARED!" on the front page of the newspaper, we began to hear reports of skirmishes across the country, and not long after that the Kemalans arrived in the neighbouring town.

Those next few days were terrible. The Kemalan army swept through the town like a ravenous plague of locusts, taking whatever they wanted and arresting anyone who got in their way. Families were displaced to make room for the soldiers, streets were blockaded to create checkpoints, buildings were vandalised to install firing positions and food was stolen and consumed even as starving youngsters looked on.

It was not long after their arrival that they discovered my father's dairy farm and when they did, there was no stopping them. They consumed my father's products voraciously; every drop of milk, every scrap of cheese he produced was taken to further the "war effort". And through all this they gave nothing back, not a penny crossed my father's palm in reparation for everything they had taken from us.

The Kemalans had quickly affected a chokehold on the entire community and no one could see any way out of it. If you were caught trying to leave the town, you were at best arrested or at worst beaten. Other such offences were punished just as harshly. The father of one my best friends was caught stealing food from a bakery the Kemalans had seized. He had only been trying to feed his family, but when the soldiers captured him, he was beaten so savagely that he had been hospitalised for days.

And their brutality did not stop there. After they had been in the town for about a week, and there had been no sight or sound of the Altegans, the Kemalan soldiers began to get bored. The worst amongst them, the truly sick and depraved ones, began to rape the female townspeople. They would take them from their homes in the dead of night, while their children and husbands fought uselessly against them, and have their way with them.

This went on for some time and would have continued unknown to most of us if their superior officers had not caught wind of their offences and made an example of them in front of everybody. An enforced meeting was called in the centre of town and when everyone was assembled the leader of the battalion stood up before us and apologised on behalf of his men.

He said that this was not how his company had been trained to behave and he was ashamed of all those involved. He promised us that it would not happen again and for a moment I almost believed him. But I detected the insincerity behind his words. Whatever he may say, he could not control every one of these animals.

To my surprise, he then led out all those men identified as the rapists and announced that they would be punished for their crimes. I think he wanted to show us that crime would not be tolerated – from civilians or soldiers – but he seemed to neglect the fact that they had been stealing from us ever since they got here. Stealing in the name of the "war effort" is – after all – still stealing.

The men were then blindfolded and positioned against a wall, and it was only as a group of soldiers standing before them raised their rifles that I realised what was happening.

It was a firing squad.

I wanted to look away, but something held my gaze and I watched numbly as the commander of the squad barked out his commands.

'Ready!'

I could not stop staring. My eyes were locked on the scene.

'Aim!'

I wanted to flinch away, to hide my face, but I was frozen.

'Fire!'

Just as their weapons beat out a tattoo of gunfire, my father turned my head to face him and kept his hands pressed against my cheeks.

'You don't want to see this,' he told me, and though I could not see it, I could still hear the gunshots and the screams of the men as they died. Those sounds will stay with me forever.

After that things got a little better, insofar as things can get better when your town has been overrun and your food supply is being bled dry by an insatiable horde. There were no more rapes – that I heard of – but crimes were still harshly punished.

I have been forced to grow up very fast in this last month. I have seen things that people twice my age should not have to see. I have been thrust into a world of misery and suffering of which I had no comprehension until now. That people can treat others like this makes my heart sink and my blood run cold.

To go from my sheltered lifestyle to this world of fear has been the most terrible surprise of my life. I can liken it to jumping into an icy pool; first comes the shock as your new situation surrounds you. Next comes the adjustment as you learn and adapt to its boundaries. And finally comes acceptance, as you become numb to everything around you.

I am already becoming numb to everything that is happening and that scares me more than anything else that has happened so far…

September 3rd 1942

I am so angry I am afraid of what I will do. I have never felt this way before. It is all consuming. I feel it growing inside me and I do not like it one bit. I need to get my feelings down on paper. Perhaps one day someone will read this; someone in power, someone with compassion, someone who will realise what this ridiculous war is doing to the people.

This war needs to end. Neither side is gaining anything from it, but the people are losing everything. We are statistics to the decision makers, acceptable collateral damage. While they hide behind their statistics, they can convince themselves that what they are doing is OK. If they could actually see it in person, if they could read the words of someone caught in the middle of it, they might realise the error of their ways and put a stop to all of this.

I have to get my words to someone in command. I have to stop incidents – like what recently happened to my father – from ever happening again. I do not want to talk about it, but I must if I want people to understand.

A couple of days ago my family and I had all but reached our limit. We had exhausted our meagre food supply and every shred of food my father produced was still being taken to feed the soldiers – taken from our open mouths. We were slowly starving to death and when my father tried to point this out to the soldiers who came by each day to collect the food, he was greeted with insults and threats.

My father was becoming a shadow of his former self. Gone was the smile that used to greet me each day. Gone was the twinkle in his eye I used to love so much. He had stopped eating completely and would force us to eat his rations, telling us that he wasn't hungry and that we needed it more than he did. He was wasting away and becoming weaker and weaker by the hour.

Last night my father decided he had had enough and went to the storehouse where the food was kept for collection. He took just enough to feed us for the next few days – hoping against hope that the deficit wouldn't be noticed – but as he was leaving the store he was spotted and captured by some soldiers out on patrol.

I was in bed at the time but I awoke at the sound of scuffling, raised voices and yells of pain. I ran to my bedroom window and looked out into the farmyard to see my father lying on the floor, surrounded by four burly men. They were beating him mercilessly, kicking him with their heavy boots and laying into him with the butts of their weapons.

One soldier stood by awkwardly, trying to control the other men and stop their attack, but they ignored him completely. Out of my mind with fear, I rushed into my parents' room and woke my mother and together we ran downstairs to his rescue.

When the soldiers saw us coming they gave him one last kick each and one of them said, 'You don't steal from us,' before they moved off and left the farmyard.

We ran to my father's side and my mother cradled his head in her lap. His face was bruised and he was bleeding from innumerable injuries as he held up the basket of food that the soldiers had – after all that – forgotten to take from his iron grip.

'Who's hungry?' he asked though gritted teeth.

I kissed him on the cheek. He is the bravest man I have ever known. He sacrificed his safety and wellbeing just to get us some food. Working together, my mother and I helped him stand up and led him inside where we spent the rest of the evening tending to his wounds.

It seems that this war is getting to everyone. Some of these soldiers are out of control. Someone in charge, someone behind all this, needs to step up and take control of their men. If they will not end this war, then they at least need to control their pawns.

September 14th 1942

I do not know what is making me put pen to paper. I think it is the only way I will be able to make any sense of this. For anyone who may be reading this, I am sorry if you find my handwriting illegible, I cannot stop the tears hitting the page. I will try to get a grip on myself just long enough. I want this to be chronicled as accurately as possible so that the people responsible will know the full tragedy of what has occurred. This is the hardest thing I have ever had to write, but I will try my best.

It finally happened. What the Kemalans had been waiting for – and some of them praying for – finally happened. Last night (or it could have been the night before, I'm not sure, I've lost track of the days) the Altegans attacked the town. The first thing we heard of it was booming gunfire in the distance and when we ran to the upstairs windows we saw flashes and explosions coming from the town square. Screams and yells could be heard even at this distance and it was not long before the night sky was lit up by a raging inferno somewhere in the town.

Smoke soon filled the air and the buildings were thrown into stark relief by the flickering blaze. Together with my mother and father, we huddled in that upstairs room, where we had a good view of the approach to the farm in case any soldiers came in our direction.

It was an awful thing to witness. As I stood at that window I watched aghast as buildings crumbled before my eyes; family homes and businesses reduced to so much rubble. I prayed that no one had been inside them when they fell. My father tried to distract me by playing card games, but every fresh sound would draw my eyes back to that terrible sight.

Would they come to our farm? That was the question; the question that led to so many others. *If they did, would they capture us? Or kill us and reduce our home to wreckage? Should we leave? Abandon the only home we've ever known? Or fight to protect what's ours?* As we sat there pondering these questions, my father suddenly got up and approached the window, his face grim and serious.

I moved next to him and followed his gaze and saw at once what he had spotted. Soldiers were marching up the road towards our farm. I could not tell if they were Altegan or Kemalan, but either way my father took action.

'Downstairs! Downstairs, both of you!' he commanded, and we hurried down to the kitchen. My father rushed to a corner cabinet and drew out a rifle he used to hunt game.

'What are you going to do?' my mother asked. 'You're not… you can't be serious!'

'Deadly,' my father replied. 'Now come on you two, get over to the hayloft and hide yourselves! I won't ask you again.'

'Just come with us!' my mother pleaded. 'Come and hide with us. You don't have to do this!'

'My family has farmed this land for generations,' my father replied. 'I'm not giving it up without a fight, and I will never let them hurt you. I'll distract them long enough for you to hide yourselves, now get going!'

My mother was torn. She stood there, rooted to the spot, unwilling to move, knowing that it was best for me but hating herself for even thinking of leaving her husband. When she still did not move, my father moved towards her and kissed her passionately on the lips, then bent down and kissed me on top of my head.

'Go, now!' he said, his eyes filling with tears that I knew he would not let fall. 'Go!'

We left then and ran across the yard towards the barn, both of us blinded by tears. We climbed together into the hayloft and lay down upon a soft blanket of hay. From our vantage point we could see the whole farmyard through a crack in the wall.

We watched as my father walked, tall and proud, across the farmyard towards the advancing soldiers. From this distance it became obvious they were Altegan, but in the end it did not matter.

They yelled at him to drop his weapon, but he would not obey. They raised their weapons and so too did he, firing off round after round into his assailants. Several of them fell, but not before my father's body was riddled with bullets. He continued bravely on for as long as he could until he could stand it no more and collapsed to the ground.

My mother could not stop crying and all I could do was stare as tears slid silently down my cheeks. I changed that day. We both did…

CHAPTER 11
The River

Breakfast the next morning was a silent affair. Marco had slept fitfully and I had not slept at all. A combination of the shocking murders we had witnessed the night before, coupled with the distressing entries I had read in Isabella's diary, had prevented me from getting even a wink of sleep. Indeed, the thought of sleep had not even entered my mind. I doubted whether I would ever be able to sleep again.

I looked over at Marco as he quietly toasted bread over the small fire we had built. I was worried about him. I had known him long enough to know that if he was not talking then there was definitely something wrong. I had expected him to bounce back from this as quickly as ever, but as the minutes dragged by without a word, I began to realise that there would be no bouncing back this time.

Perhaps leading him from his hiding place had not been the best thing for him. My decision to do so had been based on... well, nothing. From everything he had told me, it seemed obvious that his parents had been captured or worse, but I did not know that for certain. For all I knew, they could have arrived home – desperate to see their son – and found that he was gone.

What had I done…?

As doubt overcame me so too did fear and I realised that I was in the middle of nowhere with no idea what I was doing. I had taken on a passenger for my task with no prior experience of looking after anyone. I had a long journey ahead of me with only a vague idea of direction, few supplies, and a young boy who was rapidly spiralling downwards.

What on earth was I doing out here?

This was too much for me to handle. I had bitten off far more than I could chew. Everything about this situation was alien to me and I had come too far to just go back. And even if I did, what would I be going back to? There was nothing left for me back home. The only things I had left in the world were Ada, the diary, and the belief that returning the diary to its owner was the right thing to do. I would just have to hold onto that thought and keep pressing onwards as long as possible.

Marco was staring blankly into the fire and had not noticed that his toast was beginning to burn.

'I'd take that out of the fire before it turns to charcoal,' I said, trying to raise a smile. He shifted position and pulled the toast away from the heat, but he did not laugh nor even look at me. I passed him a half-empty jar of preserves we had taken from his house and he began to spread it on his toast with the same dull, listless expression on his face. I could think of nothing to cheer him up, so I looked over at Ada who was barking excitedly at something.

She was prancing round the base of a tree, staring up into the branches and woofing fit to burst. I followed her gaze upwards and saw what she was looking at. A squirrel was perched on the branch above her, nonchalantly chewing an acorn, confident of its safety.

'That squirrel's asking for trouble,' I said lightly. 'If Ada catches it she'll knock it down a peg or two.' Another squirrel appeared in the branches above the first, saw Ada, and dashed up higher. The first squirrel looked up casually then went back to its acorn.

'Now look, its showing off in front of its friends,' I said. Marco looked up too.

'I know what you're trying to do,' he said quietly. I shrugged my shoulders.

'Well, I've got to do something,' I said. 'I've never known you this quiet before.' Marco drew his knees up under his chin and began to slowly rock back and forth.

'I miss my parents,' he mumbled. 'I just want to go home.' Guilt cut through me like a knife and I was forced to turn my face away for fear of him seeing my reaction.

'I… I don't think that's the best idea,' I replied. 'You know how close we were to getting caught. You know there's military activity back there. If we go back now, we'll… we'll just be walking right into their hands. Our best bet is to keep on moving and if we do that, I'm sure we'll find your parents in the end.'

'If you think that's best,' he answered sombrely. 'I'll… I'll trust you.'

Another stab of guilt.

What had I done to earn his trust? For what possible reason was he putting his faith in me? I had led soldiers to his hiding place. I had killed a man in his home. I had then led him away from his home – the one place where his parents would know to find him should they return. I had then almost led him into a radioactive zone and made him a witness to a gruesome massacre. As far as taking care of people went, I was doing a pretty lousy job so far.

In order to get out of my own head I stood up and dusted myself down.

'We should get moving,' I said, glancing towards the river and steeling myself for what I had to say next. 'What I'm about to suggest, you're… you're not going to like.'

'What is it?' Marco asked warily.

'We need to get across this river,' I replied. 'And the only way I can see to do that is to use the…'

'No!' Marco cut across me. 'We can't… we can't use… *their* boat…'

'We have to, Marco, it's the only way we're going to be able to continue. Our only other option is to stay here… or go back.' He looked at me and in his eyes I saw reflected back the same fear I felt. I did not want to do what I was planning to do, but I could see no alternative. We could search for a bridge, but… how long might that take?

'Alright,' he said, standing up and shifting nervously on the balls of his feet. 'But let's just get it over with quickly.' I nodded and together we packed up our camp and left the forest.

In the light of day the river looked even more ferocious than I had imagined. The water was dark brown and impenetrable and the current was incredibly strong, whipping by at a tremendous pace. Here and there rocks jutted from beneath the surface and clouds of spray were kicked high into the air, causing little rainbows in the mist.

As we drew near the boat, Marco began to hang back and to be honest I did not blame him. From this distance I could see that there were four bodies lying prone in the mud and water and as we got closer still, I could see pools of blood surrounding them. I took a deep breath to try and steady myself, but it did not make it any easier. Only a few hours earlier these men had been alive and well and now they were here… and perhaps their bodies would never be claimed.

Marco had stopped moving completely and was standing stock still. All the colour had drained from his face and his eyes were wide and staring as he took in the full horror before him. I rushed to his side and clapped my hand over his eyes.

'Don't look,' I said. 'Just… just cover your eyes and I'll lead you to the boat.'

'All… alright,' Marco replied, putting his hands over his eyes.

I took him by the arm and began to lead him cautiously between the bodies, trying as much as possible to keep him from stepping in the blood. But this was an almost impossible task; it had spread so far and so wide that I could not prevent it. At one point he slipped and almost fell, but at the last second I managed to catch him and get him back on his feet. My sense of relief on catching him was immense, for if he had fallen… I believe he would never have recovered from it.

The memory of walking past those bodies is something I will never forget. For some reason I kept expecting them to move and the thought that they might terrified me. I still do not understand why. If they had moved, that would mean they were alive, and I could help them. But – fuelled as I was by fear and adrenaline – if they *had* moved, I would more than likely have just run a mile, screaming.

We reached the boat and I steadied it for Marco as he climbed inside, one hand still pressed firmly over his eyes. Ada was sniffing the bodies nearby. I called her over and motioned for her to jump into the boat. I had expected her to be against the idea but she leapt inside at once and sat at the prow, staring out across the river with her tongue lolling.

I made a quick inspection of the boat and noticed a bullet hole low down in the hull. We would not get very far if we did not plug that somehow.

'Marco,' I said gently. 'You can open your eyes now, but just keep looking straight ahead.' Marco did as I asked and stared fixedly at a point on the other side of the river.

'Now, there's a hole just down by your left foot that I need you to plug with your hand,' I continued. 'If we don't plug it this will be the shortest boat ride in history,' I added, with a weak laugh. I noticed the corners of Marco's mouth turn up in a half smile, but he did not say anything.

'You OK with that?' I asked. Marco nodded. He got down onto his knees and used the flat of his palm to cover the hole.

Before casting off, I took one final look around me. I was torn. Leaving their bodies like this felt wrong, but for one thing I was petrified of touching them, and for another I would need help moving them, and I could not ask Marco to do so. The longer we stayed here, the worse it would get for him.

My family was not religious but, given the circumstances, the only thing I could think to do was to offer up a quick prayer for the souls of the departed and wish them better luck in the next life. I prayed too that the families of the deceased would one day discover what happened to their loved ones, so they would find peace and move on with their lives.

With this, I turned back to the boat and began to push it into the water. Once it was out deep enough, I jumped inside, grabbed the oars and began to row us across to the other side.

I had only ever done this once before on a tranquil pond, so the change in pace was dramatic. I had thought the current looked fast from the bank, but out on the water it was stronger than I could have possibly imagined. Within seconds of leaving the bank we had already been swept way downriver as I strove to keep us moving towards the opposite side.

By the time we were halfway across, I was already tiring and beginning to question my judgement once again. I was so focussed on keeping the oars sliding in and out of the water that I did not notice my feet becoming wet. It was Marco who alerted me to this fact.

'Hey,' he said quietly. 'Hey, er… I think we're sinking…'

'We… what..?' I asked, doing a double take.

'We're sinking,' he repeated, indicating the water pooling around us.

'But that's not…' I began to say as I scanned the hull. Then I noticed several bullet holes below the water line that I had not spotted on my initial inspection.

'Damn… I… I should have seen them,' I said hopelessly. Water was pouring in fast and within seconds it was above our ankles. There was no way we could plug all the holes and still make it to the other side.

'We'll have to swim for it,' I said, gauging the distance to the opposite bank. 'It's not that far.'

'For you, maybe,' Marco replied. 'But I, er… I can't swim…'

I tried to control the rising waves of panic, but it was becoming too much. My head flicked between

Marco and Ada. I literally held his life in my hands. I was sure Ada could swim the remaining distance unaided, but if I did not do something soon, Marco would die, and it was likely I would join him.

The water was now close to slopping over the sides. It was time to make a move.

'Come here,' I said, and Marco came and stood mutely at my side as the boat became fully submerged beneath us. Using my left arm, I gripped him under both arms and struck out for the shore. With an excited bark, Ada leapt forward and began to swim towards the bank.

As we swam the current tugged at us like a living thing, clawing at our limbs with lithe, strong fingers. It wanted to drag us down beneath the surface. It wanted us to enter the darkness and the silence of the riverbed. It mocked us as we fought against it, playfully splashing us with water one moment, then sending us towards a rock the next.

The riverbank seemed so distant and as I desperately paddled with my right arm, it only seemed to move further and further away. My legs felt like they were made of iron and my clothes were like chain mail, dragging me down. I did not think we were going to make it.

But little by little, we began to edge our way closer to the bank until I could almost reach out and touch it. Ada had already reached the bank ahead of us and stood looking expectant, her head on one side. Marco – who until now had been almost limp in my arms – scrabbled for the bank and gripped a clump of grass. He tried to haul himself out but the grass came loose and he fell backwards. I only just grabbed him in time before he was swept away.

Using the last of my strength, I helped him climb up onto the bank and then set about clambering up myself. But my body felt so heavy and so tired and my fingers were so cold and stupid that I could not get a firm grasp on anything, and with a strangled cry I slipped backwards and fell into the water.

My head sank beneath the surface and my ears were filled with the deep, low rushing of the water. I could almost hear that insidious current laughing at me, exultant in the knowledge that it would at last claim me for its own.

I struggled to reach the surface and my head broke through, allowing me to swallow a huge lungful of air. In that moment I saw Marco – with Ada at his heels – running along the riverbank beside me, yelling at the top of his voice, desperate for a way to save me. I sank once again, pulled inexorably downwards by a force of supernatural power.

This is it, I thought. *This is how I'm going to die. This is how my journey will end.*

No! I screamed inside my head, bubbles rushing from my mouth, *it will not end this way!*

I kicked hard towards the surface and broke through again and saw Marco up ahead. A lightning-struck tree was hanging out over the water at a crazy angle, and Marco had shimmied out as far as he dared and now hung almost upside down, reaching out towards me and yelling at me to, 'Grab my hand!'

I held both my arms out of the water, grasping desperately for his hand, but as I did so the current began to pull me down again. As my face dipped below the water, I knew that I had missed my one chance at rescue.

But then I felt his hand grasp mine and he began to drag me towards the bank, displaying a strength I would not have credited him with. As though landing a fish, he fairly flung me up onto the bank and I lay there, gasping and spluttering and soaked to the skin. Ada came and sat at my side, blissfully unaware that I had almost died.

When I had coughed up what must have been several pints of water, I sat up and looked over at Marco with a newfound respect. I had been envious of his veneer of bravery, then somewhat shocked to discover the scared little boy within. Now I saw him as a person of real courage. He had saved my life, and I was indebted to him for it.

Perhaps I was not the most responsible person. Perhaps taking care of someone was not something I would ever be good at. I could barely even make decisions for myself, let alone for someone else. But it seemed that with this friendship – with this boy I had taken responsibility for – I had found someone upon whom I could truly rely.

I flopped back upon the grass and shut my eyes as I sought to regain my breath.

'Thank you,' I murmured. 'Thank you…'

CHAPTER 12
The Warplanes

My thoughts were swirling like a whirlpool and when I stood up I was unsteady on my feet. Even after lying prone for half an hour, I still felt the phantom current pulling at me, dragging me this way and that. I stumbled and almost fell, but Marco caught me and helped me remain upright.

'Maybe you should lie down a little longer?' he suggested. I shrugged him off and whistled at Ada to follow us.

'I'm fine,' I replied. 'We need to keep moving.' Marco looked at me doubtfully but did not say anything else.

After checking I had not lost anything from my bag and reassuring myself that the diary had not suffered too greatly from being dunked underwater, we set off together, continuing our westward march towards who knows what. My tangled thoughts needed time to settle, so I contented myself with drinking in the glorious scenery surrounding us. For several hours we walked, speaking very little and instead admiring the simple charm of the landscape. After such an inauspicious start to the day, those few hours felt strange and somehow peaceful. I think perhaps I was just happy to be alive.

Rolling green fields stretched out in all directions, broken here and there by a fence, a river or a line of trees. The sun hung high above it all, watching over the world like a proud parent. Clouds scudded aimlessly across the sky, casting patterns of light and shadow over the grass.

I was so absorbed by the beauty around me that at first my mind did not register the harsh lines and drab colours of a city on the horizon. It was only when I refocused – as though coming out of a trance – that I noticed it and pointed it out to Marco.

'Any idea what that city is?' I asked.

'No, I was hoping you could tell me,' he replied.

'Hmm, well anyway, it's our best bet,' I continued, changing course slightly. 'Maybe someone there will be able to help us find your parents.' At this, Marco's face lit up momentarily, then clouded over once more. I knew what he was thinking – had war visited here too?

It was early afternoon by the time we arrived on the outskirts of the city. A large, ornate sign by the roadside declared that we were now entering "Portolo". I had never been here before but from what I had read, Portolo was a bustling metropolis – inhabited by people of all nationalities. It was a popular holiday destination and as such, had been dubbed, "the sleepless city".

We had not even passed the sign yet and my heart was already racing. I knew what I expected to find here. The same thing I had found in every other town or village I had passed through… evidence of war. Would there be anyone left in this city to help us? Or had war struck this place and driven them from their homes too?

I was nervous about entering the city. Everything seemed so quiet. I was not sure I would like what we might find. But we did not have a choice. Our supplies were running very low – we needed to pick up fresh food and water. I squared my shoulders.

'Come on, Marco,' I said, trying to inject as much reassurance into each word as I could. 'Let's take a look.'

With Ada bounding along at our heels, we continued on down the road – hesitantly at first – but gradually growing in confidence as it became clear that the city had not been attacked. Or at least if it had, it had somehow avoided taking any damage in the process, for we saw no signs of bullet holes or mortar fire.

In fact, it was not long before we saw people hurrying to and fro, but not in a fearful way – in a normal, occupied, business-like kind of way. As we got further into the city, I began to wonder if these people even realised there was a war on. Everybody seemed to be going about their daily lives as though they had not a care in the world.

After only a few minutes of this, I could stand it no longer and I hailed a large, pompous-looking man who was strolling past me with a heavy bag in one hand.

'Excuse me!' I said, loudly and insistently. The man stopped and blinked at me owlishly, as though he was not used to being disturbed from his routine.

'I… I'm not quite sure how to say this, but… the inhabitants of this city are aware there's a war going on… right?' I asked. The man stared at me as though I was completely deranged.

'Why yes, of course…' he replied in bewilderment. 'How could you not be aware?' I struggled for a response, suddenly feeling very foolish.

'It's just that… everyone's going around as normal,' I continued awkwardly. 'No one seems nervous or frightened… and the city could be attacked at any moment!'

'Oh, no,' the man replied. 'That's quite out of the question. No, Portolo is under the protection of the Kemalan army. They've been using our city for quite some time now to refuel and resupply, and to some extents relax, I believe.'

'So… this city has sided with the Kemalans..?' I asked.

'Well, I can't speak for everyone else of course, but I for one *loathe* the Kemalans,' the man replied with a passion. 'They take what they please and don't give a damn about the honest citizens who live in this fair city! Why, only the other day I was evicted from my lodgings in order to make room for a new platoon. Fortunately I was able to make alternative arrangements or I would have been right up the creek. No, you'll find that most people around here hate the Kemalans and I think everyone will agree that the only good thing about them being here is that the Altegans would not *dare* attack this city while they hold it. So it may not be perfect, but at least we're not getting shot at.'

The thought that we might have found a safe haven – even for a few moments – was heartening, but I could not help thinking that it was too good to be true...

'How sure are you that we're safe from attack here?' I asked. 'I've seen the Altegans attack a lot of towns...' The man looked at me sadly as though I was completely naïve – like a toddler unable to comprehend.

'My dear boy, here in this city you are safe as houses!' he replied. These words did not fill me with confidence when I recalled the ruined buildings in Marco's home town and my own. 'There are so many Kemalans stationed here and it is so easily defensible that the Altegans would not dare risk sending troops against it,' he continued. 'You are perfectly safe, I assure you.' The man checked his watch and glanced up as though he had just seen someone he recognised.

'Well, must dash,' he said, tipping his hat to us. 'Cheerio.' And with that he was gone, vanishing around a corner quick as a whip.

Marco and I were left standing there somewhat agape. Could it possibly be true? Would we be able to rest easy tonight? The strange arrangement between the citizens and the Kemalans – a grudging acceptance of their presence in return for supposed safety – did not sit well with me. It was a similar scenario to the one outlined by Isabella, and I knew how that had ended… Wherever the Kemalans went, war and imprisonment followed… how long before it happened here too?

It seemed prudent to remain on our guard but, given the circumstances, it was the perfect opportunity to ask the locals if there were any Kemalan prison camps in the area, for I was fairly certain that if Marco's parents were anywhere, they would be in one of the nearby camps.

I voiced this thought to Marco and together we set off to explore the city and search for information.

The sun beat down mercilessly as we strolled along the city streets and it was not long before we were both drenched in sweat and desperate for a drink. As we walked we asked our question of passers-by, but they either didn't know or simply ignored us.

As bone weary as we were, it did not detract from the majesty of the city we now found ourselves in. The architecture was quite unlike anything I had ever seen before. It was a complete mish-mash of different styles co-existing side by side, but somehow it just worked. One moment we would be walking by a flamboyant mansion painted in gaudy colours and the next we would find ourselves staring at a humble little home with a thatched roof, but neither one of them seemed out of place.

Perhaps it was the different races and creeds who inhabited the city that allowed these varied styles to work together. There were so many types of people from all walks of life – living and working side by side – that these different architectural styles just seemed to make sense.

These musings carried me further down the street and I found myself standing before a gothic cathedral, replete with stone gargoyles glaring down at the citizens below. It is said that gargoyles – or to use their correct term, "grotesques" – are intended to ward off evil spirits. Looking at these grotesques, however, with their features eroded away by time and the elements, it seemed plain to me that this cathedral needed a more powerful deterrent.

I returned from the depths of my thoughts just as Marco ambled back to me, looking dejected.

'I just asked that couple over there if they knew of any Kemalan prison camps nearby and they had no idea,' he said. 'In fact, they seemed a little surprised there would be camps at all. I don't think they're from around here…'

He kicked a stone absentmindedly and looked up at the grotesques crouched on the edge of the cathedral above.

'Are you sure my parents will have been taken to one of these camps?' he asked. I struggled to find an answer to this. Of course I wasn't *sure* they had been taken to a camp, but the thought that they might be close by seemed to have invigorated Marco, and I did not want to destroy that.

'That would be my guess,' I replied. 'When the Kemalans attacked my village they took a lot of prisoners and marched them off to the camps. It's not hard to believe that the same thing might have happened in your town.'

'If they are there, we'll find them. We'll find them and we'll rescue them!' Marco said. Naïve though it may be, I was pleased to hear the same bravery in his voice that I had detected when we first met. I knelt down to stroke Ada as I thought of a response.

'Yeah, we will. Don't worry about that,' I replied, trying to sound as confident as possible. 'You feeling hungry?' I asked, seeking to change the subject.

'More thirsty than hungry,' Marco answered.

'Then let's find somewhere to get a drink,' I said. 'I could do with a rest. Come on, Ada.'

We stopped at the first café we came across and it was only then that I realised I didn't have any money. Feeling slightly foolish, I confessed this to Marco. Without saying a word, he reached into his pocket and drew out a handful of cash.

I stared at him aghast.

'Where did you get all that money from?' I asked.

'I know where my parents hide their rainy day fund,' he replied, giving me a roguish smile.

While Marco got us a table under the awning outside, I went up to the counter and ordered a couple of ham sandwiches, two bags of crisps and two glasses of lemonade. I also asked for a bowl of water for Ada and when the woman behind the counter saw her, she gave me a bright smile and said she would bring it right over. I thanked her profusely, paid what I owed and took the tray back to our table.

We had not even started eating when the woman arrived and set the bowl down in front of Ada. As she watched her noisily lap it up she stroked Ada's neck with the same smile on her face.

'What's her name?' she asked.

'Ada,' I replied quietly. I tried to think of something else to say, but I had never been very good at small talk.

'She's a beautiful dog,' the woman continued. 'If you need anything else, just shout,' she added as she walked away.

'Thank you,' I called after her.

We started eating our sandwiches. Ada was looking at me hopefully, so I fed her the crusts and she wolfed them down.

I had not taken more than a few bites when I heard a strange sound overhead. It was a high-pitched droning, like the buzzing of a million bees flying in a tight-knit group. I could not place the sound and so I walked out from under the awning – accompanied by the other customers – and together we looked up into the sky.

The sight that greeted us and the shadow that passed over us were enough to chill the blood in our veins.

Warplanes!

The Altegans had sent warplanes to attack the city!

We barely had time to dive for cover before the first bomb impacted with the pavement a couple of hundred metres away, sending shattered cobblestones zipping in all directions. The second fell much closer and a man standing nearby was struck by shrapnel and instantly killed. His lifeless body tumbled to the floor and lay still, his head twisted at an impossible angle.

Terrified screams rent the air as more bombs peppered the city and the shrill, eerie whine of an air raid siren provided a chilling backdrop to the din. Smoke and dust filled the air and within seconds we could not see our hands in front of our faces.

I grabbed Marco's arm in one hand and gripped Ada's scruff in the other, and set off running. I had a vague idea that I was heading towards the outskirts of the city, but in that moment I was driven more by instinct than conscious thought.

Vague figures flashed past in the haze of smoke, bent double and shielding their heads. Women and children, young and old alike, all fled in pure terror – driven by the desire to survive.

As my eyes grew somewhat accustomed, I noticed that bodies littered the street and at one point, I could have sworn I saw a young child crying over a limp shape, but I could not stop moving – both Marco and Ada depended on me.

There was a ringing in my ears and spots danced before my eyes as we ran. Bombs fell either side as though funnelling us to an unknown destination. Each time one fell, we would veer away from it only to be confronted by another and another. A chunk of concrete – blasted loose from a nearby pavement – caught me on the arm, gouging a deep cut that instantly welled up with blood.

With adrenaline coursing through my veins, I barely noticed the pain, all I knew was we needed to get to safety. But by this point we were hopelessly lost and the smoke showed no signs of dissipating.

A building loomed suddenly into view and we ducked inside it to catch our breath. As we stood there gasping, another bomb impacted with a building close by, spraying the street with lethal shards of glass.

'Where… are we going..?' Marco asked breathlessly.

'I don't know,' I replied, casting around for any road to safety. 'I don't know…'

Above the cacophony of explosions, screams and air raid sirens, I detected the sound of running footsteps getting closer and closer and soon two figures materialised on the pavement outside. It was a middle-aged man and woman – most likely a couple – and when they saw us, a look passed between them. They seemed to have reached an unspoken decision, for the woman stepped nearer and spoke to me.

'There's a bomb shelter not far from here,' she said, her voice barely audible. 'Follow us and we'll lead you there.' When I hesitated she looked at her husband.

'You can't stay here,' she said. 'This building's already been hit. It could come down any minute – come with us.' I nodded in agreement, too frightened to speak, and taking hold of Marco and Ada once more, we set off after them.

For the first few streets all went well. We followed as close as we could and the husband would periodically check behind him to make sure we were alright, but soon the distance between us began to increase and when a bomb fell on the street ahead of us, they vanished from sight completely.

Lost and exposed, I began to think that we would not make it out of this alive. But then I noticed a crowd of people heading down a side street to our right. Thankful for any kind of direction, I hurried towards them – dragging Marco and Ada after me.

We joined the back of the group and ran in step with them, instinctively ducking as more bombs fell around us. Before long it became clear that we were approaching a bunker and I mentally breathed a sigh of relief. Maybe we would make it through this after all.

For the next few hundred yards I just kept my head down and tried not to fall. Thus when the people ahead of me stopped abruptly, I did not react fast enough and crashed into the back of them. I got to my feet and looked towards the head of the group just as the bunker door creaked open on rusted hinges, pushed from within by unseen hands.

The crowd began to move inside, jostling and pushing – all honour and chivalry forgotten in the struggle for survival. We were at the back of the group and try as we might, we could not force our way forwards. Marco tried to nip past a burly-looking man and was thrown to the floor for his trouble.

At last we began to near the entrance, but from the glimpses I could catch of the space within, it looked to be filling up fast. When we finally did reach the door, the bunker was full to bursting point. The doorman looked at us and raised his index finger to indicate that one more person would fit. He tried to say something but I could not hear a word.

I was petrified, but there was only one course of action I could take. I knew that the next words I spoke could be the death of me, but I did not even think about it.

'You go inside,' I yelled at Marco.

'What about you?' he shouted back. 'I'm not going in there without you!'

'You have to,' I replied, shoving him forwards. 'When it's over, meet me at the King's Monument in the town square!'

Before he could reply, I grabbed Ada's scruff and sprinted away into the smoke. I did not know where I was going, or even if I would make it there alive.

But I ran, and waited to see where my legs would carry me.

Burning buildings lined my path on either side, the flames tinting the smoke a hellish colour. All was confusion, all was chaos. Craters dotted the road and it was a struggle to avoid falling into them in the thick smoke. A rumbling up ahead made me skid to a stop. I watched as 20mm flak cannons were rolled into view by Kemalan soldiers and began to fire up into the sky, empty shell casings tumbling across the street around them.

The noise was deafening and when I took my hand from Ada's scruff to cover my ears she disappeared into the smoke. I ran after her – all thoughts of my own safety forgotten – and caught up with her just as a bomb exploded by one of the cannons, throwing a soldier ten feet backward onto the pavement.

I grabbed Ada's scruff and began to run past the stricken soldier. But as I did so, I turned to look at him. He was bleeding from a dozen different wounds – his face contorted with pain and shock – and when he heard me run past, he stretched his hand towards me and screamed for help.

For a moment I carried on running – propelled by fear – but then I slowed and turned back to face him. Across the street I noticed his comrades huddled behind a wall of sandbags. Not one of them had moved a muscle to help their comrade and in that moment – even after everything they had put me through – I knew I could not leave him there to die.

Letting go of Ada once more, I grabbed the man by the collar of his jacket and began to pull him over to his comrades. It was slow going, for I was already exhausted, but as we neared the other soldiers, they began to yell encouragement.

'That's the way, over here!'

'Don't worry Jimmy, we'll save you!'

'You're going to pull through – trust us!'

Another bomb fell close by and I stumbled as rubble rained down upon us, but once I was within three feet of the sandbags, the other soldiers reached over and pulled the wounded man to safety.

Only one of them said anything to me, but I could not hear exactly what it was over the voices of the others. I did not see any point in staying. Still with no clear destination in mind I turned, caught hold of Ada, and set off running again.

Several minutes passed and no refuge presented itself. Then the curtain of smoke lifted briefly and I spotted a building up ahead. It was the cathedral we had passed earlier. It looked sturdy and secure and with no other alternatives, I headed towards it and leapt up the stairs to the main door.

With my chest heaving with exertion, I pushed open the door, ushered Ada inside, and shut the door behind me. I slumped to the floor and my chin fell upon my chest. Once I had regained my breath, I looked up to survey the area around me. The sight that met my eyes turned me cold.

Just what had I walked into now?

CHAPTER 13
The Field Hospital

Before I really saw the field hospital for what it was, I smelt it, and it was unlike anything I had ever smelt before. My nostrils were assaulted by the stink of infection and I could taste the iron-like tang of fresh blood on the air.

Even though I was sitting in the cavernous nave of the cathedral, I was surprised to discover that all sound seemed muffled – as if the very air was tense. As I surveyed the area I noticed that the heavy wooden pews – where good people once knelt before their Lord – had been pushed against the walls to make way for rows of truckle beds.

Upon each bed lay wounded and dying Kemalan soldiers, their moans of pain blending together to form an awful chorus. Nurses in white uniforms bustled from patient to patient, tying bandages, cleaning wounds and mopping brows. Now and then they would stop and offer whispered words of encouragement and reassurance, but in most cases these words seemed hollow. I doubted if many of these men would ever leave this place.

Here and there, armed Kemalans stood guard – their faces alert and nervous as explosions continued to echo around the city. Wary of being spotted, I sidled deeper into the nave with Ada at my side, took off my bag, and sat down upon a pile of rags.

As I sat there, absentmindedly stroking Ada, I felt all my pent-up fear and grief and anger leak out, and as it did a crushing exhaustion descended upon me. Before I could stop myself, my eyes had shut and I had fallen asleep.

I'm not sure exactly how long I lay there, but in the darkness of my unconscious it felt like many days. Gradually my sleep-addled mind became aware of a voice close by. The words were initially unintelligible, but they were enough to bring me back to the waking world. A youngish looking woman in a nurse's uniform stood looking down at me and I almost jumped out of my skin, fearful of being turned over to the Kemalans.

The woman looked flushed and she wiped her brow with a handkerchief. I tensed my body, ready to bolt at any second, as she stared at me curiously.

'Hello,' she said, 'and what are you doing here?' Her expression was not stern and I detected no trace of anger in her voice. I felt the tension in my body begin to fade away. I was still very unsure of myself and did not know quite what to say.

'There…' I cleared my throat and tried again. 'There was no more room in the bunker,' I finally replied, unable to muster up much more than that.

She continued to stare at me with an odd look in her eye. Was it pity? Did she feel sympathy for me? Or did she simply want me to get out of her cathedral?

'Your dog shouldn't really be in here,' the woman said at last.

So that's it, I thought. *She just wants me to go. I suppose having a dog in here is not too sanitary…*

I stood up to leave – my limbs heavy and uncoordinated after my impromptu nap – and signalled Ada to follow me, but the woman raised her hands soothingly and indicated that I should sit back down. She glanced over her shoulder warily then knelt down before me.

'I didn't mean you should go, you just need to keep quiet. They might not like it,' she said, indicating a nearby guard. I looked over her shoulder and nodded my understanding.

'Shift yourself a second,' she said. I moved to one side and she began to pull at the rags, tearing them into strips, and I realised that they were being used as makeshift bandages. When she had an armful she stood back up and glanced around once more.

'I'll be back soon – stay here,' she said. 'I'm Elsa, by the way.'

'Will,' I replied quietly. She smiled at me, then turned and walked back along the row of beds towards one of her patients. With nothing else to do,

I curled up beside Ada and tried to remain as quiet as possible.

As I lay there, listening to the screams and groans of the wounded soldiers, my thoughts went to Marco and my chest tightened with anxiety. Even though that bunker had been crowded with people, I had in fact left him alone, for he was surrounded by people who did not care for him; people who only cared for their own survival. In that place he was now more alone than I was.

As the bombs continued to fall I prayed that he would be alright. I knew that I would never forgive myself if he got injured, but what else could I have done? If I had not left him there, if I had tried to lead him here instead… I don't think either of us would have survived.

I think guilt is the natural reaction in these situations – guilt or blame. In my case, even though I believe I had no other choice, I still felt the pang of guilt. It is a strange thing. Why do we put ourselves through this? Why do we torture ourselves so? Perhaps guilt is a way of learning. If we feel guilty over a decision, we analyse it, look at all the other outcomes there could have been and from doing this we know – or at least think we know – whether we were right or wrong, and what we would do next time.

In that moment I tried to think what alternate course I could have taken, but I could see none better than the one I chose. Of course, we can never know for certain, and that is what propagates the guilt and gives it chance to grow and fester within us. I hoped that Marco would be alright, or I was sure the guilt would consume me.

Before I could fall deeper into these black thoughts, Elsa returned carrying a blanket and a tin mug. She checked around to make sure no one was watching, then knelt down and wrapped the blanket around my shoulders, noticing the cut I had sustained on my arm during the bombing. She handed me the mug.

'Drink this,' she said, as she began to clean and bandage my wound. 'It'll put some colour back in your cheeks. You look half dead.' The liquid was steaming in the chill air and when I tasted it I discovered that it was hot water flavoured with elderflower. I drank the whole thing gratefully and handed the mug back to her once she'd tied off the bandage.

'Hmm, you still look a little pale,' she said worriedly. She put a hand to my brow and held it there.

'I don't think you have a fever,' she continued, removing her hand, 'but you need to get some rest. I'll come back and check on you in a little while.' She stood up and returned to her patients.

The drink seemed to have done some good; I felt its warmth spreading throughout my whole body. From where I sat I could just see Elsa and I watched her as she ministered to the wounded. She was different to the other nurses. Most of them seemed cold and business-like in their work, but as I watched Elsa it became clear that she was very kind and gentle. I suddenly felt the urge to find out more about her – to discover how she came to be here.

I stood up and signalled Ada to stay as I picked up my bag. With my head down, so as to attract as little attention as possible, I made my way along the row of truckle beds to where Elsa was busy working. I moved to stand beside her and when she spotted me she started with surprise.

'You shouldn't be over here,' she whispered. 'If they spot you I'm not sure what they'll do.' I looked over at the guards, but every one of them seemed preoccupied with the bombing.

'I don't think they noticed me,' I replied.

'Well, just be careful,' she said, tying off a bandage. 'I wouldn't want anything to happen to you. If you want to come with me then stick close by and don't raise your voice.' I nodded mutely.

We moved on to the next bed and the sight that met my eyes made me baulk. The soldier lying before me was missing his left arm, torn clean off just below the shoulder. The stump had been bandaged tightly, but a red stain had begun to seep through. He lay still upon the bed, beads of sweat running down his face. Elsa ran a clean cloth over his brow and began to change the bandage.

To take my mind off this awful sight I desperately tried to think of some questions to ask her.

'Are you from their country?' I asked at last, nodding at the stricken man but unwilling to look at him again.

'No, I was born in this city,' she replied, without taking her eyes off her work. 'I've lived here my whole life.'

'Then… then why do you help these men?' I asked. 'They must have brought you nothing but trouble.'

At first, Elsa looked as though she did not know how to respond. She frowned slightly and her eyes glazed as though deep in thought. Then she turned to look at me.

'Because if I did not, I would be no better than them,' she said finally. 'And though they may have taken everything else from me, I will not let them take my decency.' She finished reapplying the bandage to the soldier's maimed arm then plumped his pillow and moved on to the next bed. I followed close behind her looking thoughtful.

'I helped a Kemalan,' I said quietly. 'He was injured when the bombs started to fall. His friends made no move to help him so… so I did.'

'And why did you help him?' she asked, turning her attention fully upon me.

'Because…' I faltered, caught off guard by the question. 'Because he was just a man. He was hurt and scared and alone, like me, and he… he was just a man…'

'You are a very brave boy to risk your life for him like that,' she said.

'I don't know if it was bravery,' I replied. 'It was just… the only thing to do.'

At that moment a bomb exploded just outside the cathedral. The walls rattled and showers of dust and debris rained down. All the nurses rushed to the bedsides to protect their patients. Elsa threw herself upon the man before her and bore the brunt of several lumps of masonry, while I huddled on the floor by the bed.

When the rumbling subsided I raised my head and looked at Elsa.

'Are you alright?' I asked in concern. Elsa stretched painfully and rubbed her neck where she had been struck.

'Yes… yes, I think so,' she replied. The man she had shielded looked up at her respectfully.

'Bless you,' he said, 'bless you for taking care of me like this.'

'Think nothing of it,' she replied.

I listened carefully and in the ringing silence I detected the absence of a sound I had already become used to.

'I think all the planes have passed by,' I said. 'Maybe the bombing has stopped.' Elsa listened carefully for several seconds then nodded in agreement.

'I think you might be right,' she said. 'I can't hear them anymore.'

I was about to ask her something when I realised what this meant. I had to move fast, I had to make sure he was alright! I set off running, but had only gone a few steps before Elsa called after me.

'Will! Will! Where are you going?'

I turned. It did not seem right to just leave like that, after all her kindness. I turned and walked quickly back to her.

'I'm sorry,' I said. 'It's just... I need to go check on my friend and make sure he's alright.' I set off again, but this time she caught me by the arm and held me back.

'Wait, you can't just go running off – you don't know that it's safe yet! Talk to me, tell me what's going on.' I looked around hurriedly, unwilling to waste any time, but I knew that I owed her an explanation.

'I came here with a friend – a young boy called Marco I met in a village to the east. His parents had gone missing and I found him when I hid in their cellar from Kemalan soldiers. I... I almost got him killed too, and after that I felt kind of responsible for him. So I took him with me and said I'd help him find his parents and we've been searching ever since. I reckon if... if they're not dead then they must have been captured by Kemalan soldiers and they're probably being held in a prison camp somewhere around here, but I don't know of any in the area. We've been asking around so we can go and try to rescue them.'

Elsa was giving me a sideways look, as though sizing me up. Then she shook her head.

'I don't like it,' she said. 'It's far too dangerous out there for two young boys and I feel like you aren't telling me something.' I fidgeted nervously and rubbed my arm.

'Well...' I began slowly. 'There is more to it than that. After I was first captured by the Kemalans, I found... I found this.' I reached into my coat, then hesitated.

'I've never shown this to anyone before,' I said. 'Not even Marco.'

I withdrew the diary and held it out to Elsa.

'I found it in a ditch, surrounded by dead bodies. It belonged to a girl called Isabella and… and I have to return it to her. She's been captured by the Kemalans and I know they've taken her west to their HQ in Scioli and so… that's where I'm going. I have to get it back to her – it's important! I… I just know it is…'

Elsa studied the diary closely for several minutes then stared at me as though reading something in my eyes. Then she stood up and walked over to one of the armed guards standing close by. I stayed hidden behind the bed and could just make out what they were saying.

'Excuse me, but we're running low on dried plasma,' she said. 'Do you know of any Kemalan camps in the area that we might be able to get some supplies from?'

'Of… of course,' the guard replied, clearly rattled by the bombing. 'There's a camp five miles due west of here that should have what you're looking for. I can radio for a supply run if you'd like?'

'That would be lovely, thank you,' she said with a smile. A moment later she was standing back at my side with a distinctly anxious look on her face.

'I don't like this, Will,' she said. 'I don't like this one bit. I'm worried you could get captured or worse. Is there nothing I can say to dissuade you?'

'If you knew me, you'd know that I have to do this,' I replied determinedly. 'I've taken the easy route my whole life. I've let fear rule me for far too long. I set myself this task and I'm going to finish it.' Elsa gave me one last, long look before she disappeared into the back of the cathedral.

A few minutes later she returned with several items in her hands.

'Thought you could use these,' she said, as she gently spun me around and placed them into my bag. 'There's a first aid kit, a lighter and some food and water. It's not much, but it's all we can spare at the moment. Supplies are running very low. If you ever need a place to stay, you can always come back here and find me.'

'Thank you,' I said, feeling the first sting of tears. 'Thank you for all your kindness.' I was just turning to leave when I spun back and caught her around the waist in a tight hug. She seemed a little surprised at first, but then she wrapped her arms around my neck and hugged me back.

We drew apart and I glanced at her one last time before I turned, signalled to Ada, and headed for the main door of the cathedral.

When I got outside I had to reorient myself in the ruins of this once beautiful city. The bombs had done their job and many buildings had been completely levelled. Survivors were milling about amidst the wreckage, scrounging what they could or calling for lost loved ones. I hurried off towards the King's Monument, hardly daring to believe that Marco might be there.

When I arrived my heart sank, for I could not see him anywhere. I rushed around the other side of the monument, but by this point I had already begun to suspect the worst. Then I saw him sitting on the steps and relief like I have never known flooded through me, washing my guilt away.

'Marco!' I yelled. 'Marco, it's me!' I ran towards him but he did not get up. He looked pale and frightened, but I barely registered this. I was just so happy he was alive. Ada bounded up to him and licked his face and he batted her away.

'Thank God you're alright,' I said. 'Was everything OK in the bunker?'

'It was fine...' he said hollowly, but even his tone did not register as strange with me.

'I know where the Kemalan camp is!' I blurted out. 'I think I might know where your parents are!' At this Marco's face did light up and he leapt to his feet.

'Where? Which way do we go?' he asked.

'Five miles due west!'

'Then what are we waiting for?' he said. 'Let's go! Let's go!'

THE FINAL PAGE 169

CHAPTER 14
The Rescue

Marco's excitement was infectious, but it was hard to feel it whilst walking through the ruins of Portolo. So many lives had been lost, and what had it gained the Altegans? They had not moved in to take the city in the aftermath; they had not used it as an opportunity to take control of a key staging point. They had simply done it to thin the Kemalan ranks and damage their morale, heedless of the civilian lives that would be lost at the same time.

It made me wonder again at the kind of minds that would order such attacks; the kind of people who could see civilian lives as mere statistics. How do these men sleep at night? When they are alone with nothing but their thoughts and their deeds, does it haunt them? I like to think that it does, for that would mean they have consciences, and if they do indeed have consciences then perhaps there is a chance they can be reasoned with.

I noticed that Marco had suddenly gone very quiet, his excited murmuring ceasing abruptly.

I looked up and noticed that we were passing the entrance to the bunker he had sheltered in. Something about it looked wrong, but I could not determine what it was. Something very bad had happened there, and I needed to find out what. But, rather than pressing him for an answer, I hoped that Marco would come round to telling me on his own, so for the moment I let it be.

We were nearing the edge of the city, but something held me back. Even after the horror of what had happened here, I found that I did not want to leave. My thoughts flew to Elsa and I realised that if I wanted to, I could abandon my task right now and stay with her. She had offered me a home. I could live with her and be loved by her and forget everything else.

But then I pushed the thought from my mind as fast as it had arrived. Maybe someday that could happen. Maybe someday I could live with her. But that time was not now. I had important things to do first.

Before long we found ourselves in the hills outside Portolo. From this distance the devastation was even more apparent. A great cloud of smoke hung over the city and the once beautiful buildings now resembled jagged teeth. The citizens who lived there would have a hard task rebuilding their lives from the ashes they had been reduced to, but if the people we had met were anything to go by, then it was clear that these resilient folks would be back on their feet in no time.

Marco had not said anything for some time and it was clear he would not voluntarily talk to me about what had happened in the bunker. I knew the dangers of bottling up such feelings, and I understood that the best way to deal with them was to talk it over.

'I need you to talk to me, Marco,' I said. He turned to look at me cagily. 'I need you to tell me what happened in the bunker.'

He looked away, as though he did not want me to see his face, and for a moment I thought he would not answer me. Then he turned back to me and there were tears in his eyes.

'It was horrible!' he cried, his voice breaking with emotion. 'After you left they shut the door and we all just stood there in total darkness. I couldn't move, could barely breathe. I had to listen helplessly to the bombs falling all around us, knowing that at any second one of them could fall right on top us... and one of them did!' I caught my breath as he said this and stopped dead.

'What?!' I said hoarsely. 'What happened?'

'Everyone was getting fidgety,' Marco continued. 'The bombing seemed like it was nearing its end and some people started pushing their way towards the door. One man bumped into me and knocked me to the ground and it was as I fell that a bomb hit the rear of the bunker. The whole back section of the roof caved in and... if I hadn't been on the ground

I would have been killed… Fifteen, maybe twenty people were at the rear of the bunker when it hit. I don't think… I don't think any of them survived.'

'Dear God…' I whispered.

'After that everyone scrambled for the door to escape and I was almost trampled to death. Luckily the bombing had stopped by the time we all got out, but I didn't know that… I… I just headed for the monument to meet you.' Here Marco rubbed his eyes on his sleeve. 'I didn't think I was going to make it.'

I gripped Marco's arms tightly in both hands and looked straight into his face.

'But you did make it,' I said. 'We both did, and now we're going to find your parents. You trust me, right?' Marco had been avoiding my eyes, but he looked at me then and nodded.

'Yes,' he replied. 'Yes, I trust you.'

'Then come on,' I said. 'It's only a couple more miles this way.'

About an hour or so later we were crossing a field when we spotted suspicious activity up ahead. We needed a place to watch from and a ramshackle barn nearby offered the perfect cover, so we ducked inside to hide. It was dark and cool within the confines of the barn. The wind rattled the shutters and whistled through holes in the roof. We climbed up into the hayloft and eased open a shutter to survey the area.

From this distance we could not see any faces, but it was clear what was going on. The Kemalans were using the prisoners as an improvised workforce. Men and women of varied age and race were hard at work hauling stone and digging ditches and we realised that they were building a road. The Kemalans must be in desperate need of easier access for their tanks and infantry if they were prepared to use unskilled labourers for such a task.

The movement of the prisoners was slow and awkward and then we noticed that they were shackled together like criminals. It seemed strange that the Kemalans would do this when they had not shackled me and my fellow prisoners after the attack on my village. Perhaps there had been numerous runaways? Maybe they thought it better to manacle them together and lower their work speed than risk losing them completely.

'Do you see your parents?' I asked Marco. He squinted hard then shook his head.

'We're too far away, I can't tell if it's them,' he replied.

'Alright, we'll take a closer look, but stick right behind me and keep your voice down,' I said.

We climbed down from the hayloft and crept around the outside of the barn. Between us and the Kemalans was a large expanse of field bordered by high stone walls. The field was full of unripe corn or barley and thankfully the leafy green stalks would provide some cover. Even so, we needed to cross without being spotted and in broad daylight that would be tricky.

'OK, if we're going to do this then we need to move fast and stay low,' I whispered. 'You ready?' Marco nodded silently. I took one last look around, then hauled myself up and over the wall and crouched down on the other side. Marco followed and I helped him safely down.

Holding a finger to my lips, I began to creep along between the stalks, staying as low as I could. Now and then I would poke my head up to see what the Kemalans were up to, but each time they seemed preoccupied with their prisoners.

After several tense minutes we made it to the opposite wall and put our backs against it. The Kemalans and their prisoners were now only about fifty yards away from us.

'Do you think they saw us?' Marco asked breathlessly.

'No, no, I'm sure they didn't,' I replied. 'I'll give you a boost so you can take a look for your parents.' I knelt down on the ground and Marco clambered gingerly onto my back so he could peek over the lip of the wall. For several moments he was quiet as he surveyed the workforce.

'Do you see them?' I asked at last.

'No, I… I can't see them any… wait! It's dad!' he fairly yelled. 'That's my dad over there! Hey, d-' Before he could say any more, I had yanked him to the ground and clapped my hand over his mouth.

'Keep quiet!' I hissed. 'Do you want to get us both caught?'

'But that's my dad,' Marco mumbled.

'I know, and you'll do him no good if you get captured too,' I said sternly. 'We need to think this through. If we run in without a plan we'll just get caught. Give me some time to think.'

I released Marco, then stood up and peeked over the wall to check that we had not been detected. It appeared that we had been lucky; the guards and workers continued about their business, oblivious to our presence. I scanned the area and spotted several things that caught my interest, then sat back down against the wall. I felt almost light-headed as all the doubt I had carried over leading Marco from his home slowly ebbed away. I had done the right thing. His parents had indeed been captured, now all we had to do was find a way to release them... As I pondered this I sat still and quiet and soon became lost in thought.

It had started to get dark and still the prisoners toiled on as the shadows lengthened around them. The plan I had concocted hinged on the cover of night, and it was almost time to put it into action.

Half an hour later the time was right.

'Stay here,' I said to Marco. 'And keep an eye on Ada; don't let her run after me.' Marco nodded as I hoisted myself to the top of the wall and dropped down silently on the other side.

Before doing anything else I reached into my coat and pulled out the diary. I was worried that it might fall from my pocket during the coming events, so

I decided to stash it in my bag. But first I flicked it open to a page at random and a passage immediately leapt out at me:

'While war rages the innocent will never be free. They will live in fear and doubt and pain until someone stands up and says, "No more!" or those behind the atrocities achieve their greedy aims. There are no winners in war – only casualties.'

As I read this I knew that I was not the one to stand up and say "No more!" but if I could at least do something – if I could at least help out in some small way – I would be one step closer to becoming that person.

With this in mind I thrust the diary into my bag and focussed on the task at hand.

Not far off I could see the silhouettes of the prisoners still working hard on the road and surrounding them stood the guards, rigid and motionless against the darkened sky. The wind buffeted me as it swept past, carrying their voices to my ears. The prisoners sounded exhausted and resentful and the guards bored and listless.

My eyes moved to a series of tents to the south of the half-finished road and I crawled stealthily towards them, tense and alert, ready to run at any moment. There were no soldiers standing guard over the tents. Most were watching the prisoners, but three or four were sitting around a small fire, talking quietly.

When I reached the first tent I crawled around the back and lifted up the flap to peek inside. All I saw were a couple of truckle beds and footlockers. I moved on to the next tent and found the same thing. One of them had to have what I was looking for. I moved on to the next tent and still found nothing.

When I reached the fourth tent I lifted the flap – expecting to discover more of the same – but instead found myself looking at a stack of small wooden crates, each packed tight with hay. *I had found them!*

Slowly and carefully I lifted down one of the crates, but as I turned to slide it under the flap the remaining tower of crates fell to the ground with a crash that made the guards sitting around the fire leap to their feet.

'What was that?' one of them asked.

'I dunno,' another said. 'Go check it out.' I withdrew quickly and hunched down behind the tent with the crate, hardly daring to breathe. The soldier stalked warily towards the tent and lifted the front flap to check inside. When he saw the fallen stack of crates he snorted with derision.

'It's just the crates!' he called over his shoulder. 'Frankie didn't stack 'em straight again.'

'Damn Frankie,' another said. 'I swear that kid'll be the death of us.'

I could not believe my luck. The soldier turned and moved back towards the fire and when I was sure he was out of earshot, I picked up the crate and hurried as fast as I could back to Marco and Ada's hiding place.

When I dropped down behind the wall, Marco jumped as though he had seen a ghost and clutched Ada.

'I've got it,' I said triumphantly. 'Now, you remember what I told you?' I opened the lid of the crate to reveal hundreds of rounds of ammunition packed in soft hay.

'You take the lighter and this crate and head up to the brow of that hill over there.' I pointed to a hill just to the north of the road. 'When you get there, you set light to the hay, then run as fast as you can back to the barn. Don't stop for anything and certainly don't return to the crate once it's lit. Got it?'

'Got it,' Marco replied, the spark of his old bravado evident in his voice once more.

'Then go,' I said. 'I'll see you at the barn.' Marco picked up the crate and hurried off into the darkness. I turned to Ada and held her muzzle gently in both hands. Her faithful brown eyes swept my face and all I saw in them was trust and love.

'You've got to stay here, Ada,' I whispered. 'You can't come – you might give me away. I'll find you once it's done.' I kissed her on top of the head then climbed up the wall and jumped down the other side. I could hear her whining and scratching at the wall, but I knew that she was safer there than with me.

I knew I didn't have much time before Marco's distraction would start, so I ran as fast and as quietly as I could into position. I stopped between two of the tents and looked north towards the hill.

Any second now, I thought. *Any second now.*

But nothing happened. For three or four minutes I crouched there – tense and alert – watching the hill, but seeing nothing.

I was just beginning to think that something must have happened when a faint glow appeared on the hilltop, illuminating the trees on either side. This was quickly followed by the rattle of gunfire as the burning hay ignited the gunpowder in the shells.

My eyes flicked to the Kemalan soldiers and I watched as the men around the fire simultaneously leapt to their feet and those standing guard clutched their weapons compulsively. The prisoners too stopped work and looked fearfully up at the hill. The leader of the squad began barking orders and before I knew it the entire squad, save one man, were running full pelt towards the hilltop.

This was my one and only chance, and I had to take it.

The remaining guard was standing a short distance away with his back to me. He was rocking on the balls of his feet, clearly eager to investigate; his attention entirely occupied.

I checked the area for something heavy and spotted a cast-iron cooking pot by the embers of the fire. I moved slowly towards it and gripped the handle, then began to creep up behind the guard.

Over by the road, the prisoners had begun to mill around and one of them – a young boy of roughly my age – spotted me. He pointed in my direction and began to say something out loud, but his mother – who seemed to have quickly read the situation – clapped a hand over his mouth.

But it was too late. The guard, sensing that something was amiss, turned to face me. With nothing to lose, I swung the pot anyway and caught him smack on the temple. Without a sound, he crumpled to the ground and lay still.

My hands were shaking with fear as I began to check him for keys and soon found a set attached to his belt. I quickly unhooked them and hurried over to the prisoners. The first one I came across was an elderly man who was shaking his head in amazement.

'My word, son,' he said with a smile. 'You've got some courage in you and that's for sure!'

I smiled back as I fumbled for the right key in the darkness. The first two I tried wouldn't fit, but the third clicked smoothly into the lock and unfastened the shackles.

'You've got to move fast,' I said to him. 'Head towards the old barn and from there head east and get as far away as you can.'

'Will do, son – and bless you for doing this,' he replied.

With very little time left, I moved swiftly from prisoner to prisoner, unlocking their shackles and instructing them where to run. Several of the prisoners wept with relief and gratitude and I had to ask them to keep quiet for fear of alerting the Kemalans.

Before long I had released all but one prisoner and right at that moment the gunfire ceased, the glow diminished, and a tense silence fell. My head snapped up and I watched in horror as the Kemalans descended the hill towards us, their voices raised in anger and confusion.

I had to work fast.

The last prisoner was a woman in her late thirties and, as I knelt down next to her, I realised that she was Marco's mother. He had pointed her out to me earlier when I had been formulating my plan.

'Marco's waiting over near the old barn,' I whispered, as I worked on her shackles. 'Get him and your husband and get as far away from here as possible… please!'

'I will,' she replied hoarsely, 'and thank you. Thank you!' She stood up and kissed me on the forehead then hurried away towards the barn.

I wanted to follow her, but by this point the Kemalans were almost on top of us. I watched frozen as Marco's mother raced away and I realised that I could not go with her. If I did they would track us all down and everything we had done would be for nothing.

I could dimly make out the forms of Marco and his parents as they were reunited and in the half-light of the moon I saw him wave at me, urging me to join them. For a split-second I was rooted to the spot as fear took hold. But then a single clear thought cut through it all.

I am not a coward.

Before I knew what I was doing, I was shouting at the top of my voice and running westwards, away from Marco and his parents. Behind me I heard the Kemalans yell and give chase, but I focussed on putting one foot in front of the other and not tripping over in the dark.

I was tired and frightened and I soon felt the Kemalans closing in. I risked a look behind me and saw that every one of them had given chase. I felt a smile tug at my lips. My distraction had worked.

I stumbled on an exposed root and as I righted myself a soldier tackled me to the ground. Groggy and disoriented, I felt myself being dragged back towards the road. One of the soldiers hit me and they were shouting in my face, but all I could hear was the pounding of blood in my ears.

By the time we reached the road the pounding had reduced and I overheard one of the soldiers say that they had not found the other prisoners. This elicited cries of anger from the leader and I could not stop the feeling of self-satisfaction that spread throughout my body.

The last thing I heard was the soldiers discussing a believable excuse for losing an entire workforce, then a shadow passed over me and I saw their leader standing at my side. He was holding a rifle and before I could flinch away the butt had hit me square on the jaw, and I lost consciousness.

CHAPTER 15
The Prison Camp

Blurred shapes swam before my eyes, twisting and turning like falling leaves. I tried to focus but this just made the pain worse. The inside of my head felt like a thorn bush – every tiny movement sending jagged pain rippling outwards. I became aware of voices all around me, but they were no clearer than radio static.

With a groan, I craned my neck to look up but my head seemed so heavy, and trying to move it only intensified my agony. I felt a tightness under my arms as though someone was gripping me and a sudden jolt to my kneecaps made it clear I was being dragged.

What was going on? Where was I being taken?

I could not remember what was going on or how I had got here, but one clear thought broke through the confusion.

I have to escape!

I began to struggle feebly, flailing my arms and kicking out at my captors, but this only made them grip me tighter. One of them slapped me in the face and yelled at me, but his voice was strange and distorted and I could not understand what he said.

I tried to shout for help but my voice was little more than a rasp and there was a funny taste in my mouth, like iron. Was it blood?

A shape up ahead swayed and shimmered like heat haze in the dark and gradually became clear. It was a chain-link fence, topped with razor-sharp barbed wire. A guard standing by it reached over and tugged open a heavy-looking gate, and I finally understood where I was being taken.

It was a prison camp…

I struggled harder than ever against my captors, twisting my head to try and bite their hands, but they had my arms pinioned and their grip was like iron. There was no point in fighting. I soon gave up any attempt at resistance and watched numbly as the gate slid past my field of vision and I entered the prison pen.

Before I knew what had happened, I was thrown forwards and with no chance to react I hit the dirt, my cheek bashing painfully against the hard ground. Dazed and winded, I sucked in great lungfuls of air, drawing in dust at the same time which set me coughing and spluttering.

I rolled onto my back and lay there, clutching at my chest and jaw simultaneously. There was a dampness under my fingers as I ran a hand over my chin. I raised it to eye level and saw that my fingertips were slick with blood. I felt the area again and noticed there was a raised lump, and in that moment I remembered what had happened.

I had been running. Running in the dark. Running from the Kemalans after freeing the prisoners. I had been tackled from behind and dragged back to the road. Their leader had stood at my side and then hit me with his gun. After that there was nothing… Nothing until a few moments ago.

The clearest image I could remember from earlier that night was of Marco waving at me to join him and his parents. I wish I had been able to do so. He had looked so happy. I hoped against hope that he, his parents, and the rest of the prisoners, had managed to escape safely. I guessed I would never know.

I was alone. Marco was gone, I had left Ada behind, and I was now a prisoner of the Kemalan army, doomed to serve out my days or the remainder of the war (whichever came first) as – essentially – a slave. As I lay there on my back with blood spilling down my chin, I felt the weight of failure descend upon me and every bad thing that had happened so far on my journey flooded my mind, clamouring for attention.

I raised my bloodstained hands to cover my eyes as tears threatened to fall and for a moment I saw my parents' faces before me, hazy and ethereal. I wanted nothing more than to be held by them one last time, but it was a dream that would never be realised. I felt an ache in my chest that took my breath away, and as I struggled to gulp down air their faces faded to be replaced by another.

This face was different, unfamiliar, but it was a face that told a thousand stories. Every line upon it spoke of a love lost, a hope dashed, or a secret hidden deep. It was a face sculpted by worry, grief and mistreatment. It was the face of a man who had been downtrodden for so long that he had become world-weary and cynical.

As I looked upon this shadowy face I realised that this was no vision or trick of my imagination. This was a real man of flesh and blood standing over me and, as if to confirm this, he spoke to me.

'Are you alright, boy?' the man asked anxiously. I sat up slowly and wiped my sleeve across my chin, smearing it with blood. I looked up at the man blearily. My automatic response to being asked such a question was to say "Fine", but at that moment it would have been about as far from the truth as it is possible to be.

'Not really,' I replied eventually.

'That was quite a fall you had there,' the man continued, 'it looks like they roughed you up pretty good.'

'Yeah, I think I annoyed them,' I replied as I tried to get to my feet.

'Why, what did you do?' the man asked.

'Released one of their work teams,' I said simply, my legs giving out beneath me.

'Look, just stay still, boy,' the man said, 'I don't think you should be moving anywhere for a while yet.'

I decided to listen to him and gave in trying to stand up. But as I drew my knees up under my chin

I suddenly realised that I felt considerably lighter. With a growing sense of horror, I patted my chest and back and realised what was missing.

'My bag!' I yelped, sitting bolt upright. 'They've taken my bag!'

'Well, of course they did,' the man replied in surprise. 'What did you expect?'

As the enormity of what had happened became clear I felt blood rush to my head and I began to feel woozy.

They had taken the diary!

Only a few hours ago I had put the diary in my bag for safekeeping, and now they had taken it! I tried to steady myself – to calm my thoughts and think clearly – but all I could see was them holding the diary, flicking through its pages and reading its contents.

It was not meant for their eyes!

I stood up uncertainly – ignoring the protests of the old man – and swayed on the spot as the dizziness subsided, but my heart continued to pound wildly. I had to get out of here. I had to find out who had taken the diary and get it back from them. It was the only thing that mattered any more.

I turned full circle and surveyed the area around me. It was still dark, but in the glow of electric spotlights I could discern that the Kemalans had set up camp on an old farm. Shadowy forms of outbuildings, barns and a distant farmhouse could be seen, and scattered around the yard were numerous campfires, around which sat Kemalan soldiers, warming their hands over the flames and idly chatting.

I shifted my gaze closer to home and saw that we were being held in an old horse pen, bordered on one side by a crumbling barn. There were around forty or fifty men and women standing around, and many of them were looking directly at me. I tried to ignore this fact as I continued my inspection of the area.

The flimsy wooden railings – used to keep the horses from escaping – had been reinforced with chain-link fences, topped with barbed wire. There was only one gate into the pen and it was locked with a hefty-looking padlock.

Bales of hay had been tossed into the pen for the prisoners to sit on and in one corner stood an old water butt, from which a youngish man was drawing a drink. I searched desperately for an escape route, but soon realised there were none. My frustration was only compounded by the sight of rolling green fields in the distance beyond the fence, mocking the freedom now denied me – it would have almost been better to have had no view at all.

I was pervaded by a feeling of helplessness and with nothing else to do, I sat down upon a bale of hay to try and gather my thoughts. It was only then that I realised just how exhausted I was and I could barely raise my head when the old man reappeared at my side.

'Rough day?' he asked. It was one of those questions where the answer is so blindingly obvious that it does not need asking, but I could tell that he meant well.

'You could say that,' I replied shortly. As well-meaning as he may have been, I did not much feel like talking at that moment. But the old man did not seem to pick up on this.

'Want to talk about it?' he persisted. I really *did not* want to talk about it, but something in his manner made me feel that I could trust him, and with Marco gone I had no other allies, and no one else to talk to. I held out my hand for him to shake.

'Will, William Belmont,' I said, as he took my hand and shook it firmly.

'Carlo,' the old man replied. 'Can't remember my surname, never had much use for it.' He looked at me expectantly with his eyebrows raised, as though waiting for me to speak, and when the silence became uncomfortable, I snapped.

'Yeah, I've had a rough few days,' I said at last, my words sounding laboured to my own ears. 'And it appears you have too.'

'Ahh, my story is a long and boring one,' Carlo replied, sitting down on the bale of hay next to me. 'I'm much more interested in how you came to be here, and why you're so upset over losing your bag.'

I looked up at him. This level of interest in me was an alien experience. I am not usually the kind of person people ask questions of – for nothing of interest ever used to happen to me. My natural response is to deflect a question back at the questioner, and turn their attention back on themselves, but I did not think that tactic would work here.

'Well, to use the age-old qualifier, it's a long story…' I said, hoping to deter him.

'I don't have any other plans tonight,' he said with a chuckle. And that was that.

I took a few deep breaths then launched into my story, relaying pretty much everything that had happened to me since Chotolo – only leaving out the bits that were still too painful to discuss. As I spoke it actually came as a relief to get it off my chest; to lay it all out before me, and in some respects analyse the choices I had made along the way. It was an almost cleansing experience, and Carlo made a perfect audience – he did not interrupt once and his eyes remained locked on mine throughout, his attention never wavering for a second.

Throughout the story I emphasised the importance of the diary, and when I reached the events that had led to my capture – including putting the diary in my bag for safekeeping – his eyes lit up as he realised the true source of my agitation.

When I finally finished the story, my voice had grown hoarse and I became aware that several other prisoners had been listening in. Carlo continued to stare into my eyes with a penetrating look and a thoughtful expression on his face. I tried to return his stare but before long I had to look away.

'So anyway,' I said throatily, 'that's why I need to get out of here and get my bag back.' I dropped my gaze and sat down upon the floor with my back against the hay bale.

Without a word, Carlo stood up and moved around to face me. When I looked up at him he was still giving me a considering look.

'You're young, boy, and still so full of hope,' he said at last. 'Most of us here… we gave up on hope long ago. We can help you get out and get your bag back.' My eyes widened and I looked up at him eagerly.

'Really?' I asked incredulously. 'You can do that?'

'All we need is a plan,' Carlo replied. 'And I think I have one. Michael, Vito,' he said, waving at a couple of burly looking men standing nearby, 'come over here and listen to this…'

Only minutes later – with our plan formulated – Carlo signalled for it to begin. Dawn was fast approaching and we needed to move quickly if it was going to work. I hurried into the shadow of the barn, close to the gate, and waited.

Michael and Vito – the two men Carlo had spoken to – were standing in the centre of the pen and speaking in raised voices. They began to yell at each other and Michael pushed Vito to the ground. This developed into a scuffle and before long a full-blown fight had broken out.

Several of the female prisoners screamed and this, combined with the sounds of their fight, drew the attention of the nearby soldiers. They approached the fence, but rather than jumping in to break up the fight they began to jeer and shout at the two combatants.

'Go on, hit him harder! Don't just tap him!'

'I've got a fiver on the bald one, any takers?'

'Only bit of fun we've had all day, this!'

My heart sank. It seemed that our plan had failed. These barbarians would happily watch the two men kill each other and not lift a finger to prevent it.

What the hell was I going to do now?

CHAPTER 16
The Farmhouse

As I watched Michael and Vito pummel each other under the leering stares of the Kemalan soldiers, the spark of hope that had kindled in my breast gradually dimmed. Instead, I felt shame... and remorse. These two men were giving it their all and really hurting each other just to help me, and it had come to nought.

As my mind raced between different possibilities, I looked up and spotted an officious-looking man exit a nearby building and approach. I suspected that he must be a Captain and my inspection of him would have ended there if it were not for the item he was carrying.

My bag!

It was clutched loosely in his right hand and I felt an incredible surge of rage at the sight of him holding it.

That's mine! I wanted to scream. *How dare you take it!*

In my anger I had unconsciously taken a step forward and almost revealed my position, so I quickly ducked back into the shadow of the barn as the Captain drew nearer to the pen.

When he reached the fence he turned to one of the watching soldiers and spoke to him.

'What is going on here?' he asked quietly.

'Just a bit of entertainment provided by our prisoners, Captain,' the soldier replied.

I expected the Captain to put a stop to it at once, but instead he simply stood there and watched the two men fight. I could not believe what I was seeing. *Why were they not stopping this?*

I could see that Michael and Vito were tiring and both were bleeding from a multitude of wounds. Each and every blow they landed made me wince until I was forced to turn away. There was no way they could keep at it much longer.

The Captain continued to watch for another minute, then turned back to the soldier he had addressed earlier, his expression icy.

'Private, those men look like they are about to kill each other and if that were to happen, there would be two less able-bodied men to work on the road the General ordered us to build. Unless you want to take their place in the work team, I suggest you stop this fight immediately.' I breathed a sigh of relief. Even if we had missed our opportunity, at least he would stop the fight.

'And the rest of you,' the Captain barked as the cowed soldier hurried to open the gate, 'haven't you got anything better to do?'

The other soldiers, looking sheepish, walked quickly away from the fence and tried to appear as busy as possible. With one last disdainful look at both the soldier and the fighters, the Captain turned and walked away with my bag in his hand.

The soldier, who by now looked distinctly nervous, fumbled with his keys and eventually managed to open the gate. But in his haste to break up the fight he neglected to shut it properly and, as it swung to behind him, I stuck out my foot and stopped it from closing.

As I steeled myself to run, I checked that none of the nearby soldiers were looking in my direction and – as luck would have it – none of them were. After the harsh words of the Captain, they were all performing any menial task they could find until he was well out of sight.

Taking a deep breath, I made my move. Quickly and quietly, I snuck out of the gate and scurried through the shadows of the barn wall, only slowing when a soldier passed close by my position.

Almost giddy with fear and adrenaline, I slid into the dark confines of the barn and crouched down behind a bale of hay. My heart was pounding as I waited, breathless, to see if my escape would be noticed. A minute later I heard the gate to the pen shut and lock, then silence. No calls of alarm, no angry voices; I had completed phase one of my escape. Now for the tricky part…

Cautiously, I stood up and peeked over the bale of the hay. From my position I had a good view across the farmyard and I used this chance to search for any sign of the Captain.

After a minute or so of looking, I could not see him anywhere. Panic began to rise within me as I realised what this meant. If I could not figure out where the Captain had gone, I would have to search every building to find him, and that would be incredibly risky…

As I stood there, alone and terrified, the coward within me started to whisper from the shadowy corners of my mind.

Turn back, you know they'll catch you.

Why risk it for someone you've never even met?

Next time they won't bother imprisoning you – they'll just shoot you on sight.

I tried not to listen but the voices filled my mind, blotting out all else, as though a whole crowd of people were shouting in my face. I held my head in my hands, willing the voices to stop, and just as it was becoming unbearable I spotted the Captain across the farmyard, and the voices faded to nothing.

He was walking side by side with another soldier, speaking heatedly and gesticulating wildly. He was still holding my bag and for a second I thought perhaps my escape had been noticed, but still no alarms were raised and my suspicions died away.

The two men approached the farmhouse and opened the front door. The Captain entered first, with the soldier following close on his heels, and the door slammed behind them. I now knew where he was. It was time to begin phase two of the plan.

Dawn was not far off and the shadows were rapidly shrinking. I was running out of places to hide and had to move fast. I had quickly weighed up my options and my chosen route to the farmhouse was going to be circuitous, but it was safer than taking a more direct course.

I tensed my muscles and prepared to move as I watched a guard pass by on his patrol route and disappear from view. Once he was out of sight, I ducked down and ran as fast as I could out of the barn and towards an old cart that had been abandoned at one edge of the yard.

I skidded to a stop in the shadow of the cart and checked all around. Not far away, several soldiers sat round a fire, talking in loud, slurred voices. Even from this distance I could smell the alcohol on their breath. Their discussion was base and crude and I felt sickened to even be near them.

There was no time to hang around. Checking that the coast was clear, I hurried on to my next position – a ramshackle old shed by the wall of the yard. As I ran I stumbled on a stone and almost fell, but managed to maintain momentum and enter the shadows.

This was the scariest moment so far. From where I stood I could see out across the whole yard, and for the first time I appreciated just how many Kemalan soldiers were stationed here.

On the opposite side of the yard were several barns – which had been appropriated as barracks – and I watched as men drifted in and out of them. Groups of guards stood here and there with their weapons drawn and ready and the rest sat around countless campfires, drinking and talking and laughing.

There must have been hundreds of soldiers, each one with an itchy trigger finger just waiting for the opportunity to get some target practice. I was determined not to give it to them.

At that moment a spotlight swept past my position and I just managed to avoid it in time. I looked up fearfully and spotted a guard in a makeshift lookout post at the top of an old flour mill. This was something I had not counted on. If the spotlight found me there would be no escape.

As the guard combed the area, I watched the pattern of the spotlight's movement and waited for the right moment. When it passed me again, I ducked out from the cover of the shed and used the shadow of the nearby wall to my advantage. I hurried along its length until I was parallel with the farmhouse, then broke away and made a beeline for the back door.

I had just thrown my back against the farmhouse wall when the spotlight slid past, illuminating the spot I had stood upon not a moment before. As I crouched there with my chest heaving, my senses felt infinitely magnified as adrenaline pumped through my system. The gravel under my palms felt like rocks, the campfires smelt like raging infernos and every creak from the house behind me sounded like a rifle shot.

As much as I needed to get my breath back, I knew I could not stay here. I had to keep moving. Treading carefully, I inched my way along the wall until I was below a window. Voices came from somewhere within and I cautiously raised my head to take a peek.

A picturesque little kitchen met my gaze – the kind of kitchen I always imagined you would find in a farmhouse. The cupboards and surfaces were all solid oak, there were blue and white chequered curtains framing the window, and in the centre of the room was a heavy pine table.

Family photos hung upon every wall, each one of a jovial-looking husband and wife and their young son. Most appeared to have been taken upon the farm, but several were clearly from family holidays they had enjoyed together.

I wondered what had happened to them, and where they were now…

On the opposite side of the kitchen was an open door, offering a view through the entrance hall to the living room beyond. Within it I could see the shape of a man seated in an armchair. He was talking to someone, but I could not see who it was.

I was just moving to get a better view when a soldier appeared in the doorway and headed straight for me.

Petrified, I ducked back down immediately, praying that I had not been spotted. Just above my head, I heard the sound of water running in the sink below the window and the clatter of utensils being washed. A few moments later the water shut off and the kitchen fell silent.

That was too close.

I had still not quite figured out the best route into the house, so I checked all around for inspiration. My eyes fell upon a trapdoor nearby and I realised what it meant. A cellar. I had found my way in.

The trapdoor squealed on its hinges as I eased it open, setting my teeth on edge. I was becoming careless, but I knew I had to make haste. Dawn was only a few minutes away and once it broke, my escape would become far more difficult.

As soon as the trapdoor was open I stepped inside and closed it behind me as quietly as I could.

It was pitch black within and I had to feel ahead with my toes to be certain that I wouldn't trip and fall down the stairs. As I descended further into the darkness, I tried not to think about the last two times I had been in a cellar, but try as I might, I could not stop the onslaught of images that bombarded my subconscious.

A rectangle of light from a closed door not far ahead rescued me from these thoughts and as I reached the bottom of the stairs I moved towards it with my hands outstretched like a blind man. Tables, chairs and other objects sought to trip me as I crossed the cellar and on several occasions they almost did, but soon I made it to the bottom of the stairs leading into the house and began to climb towards the shining outline above.

When I reached the top of the stairs I felt around for the door handle and soon found it. I listened for a minute or so to check that no one was nearby, then – with infinite care – I twisted the handle and inched the door open.

I froze. Across the hall from me, through the open living room door, was the man I had seen earlier, seated in his armchair, and he was looking right at me! It was a second or two before I realised that his eyes were closed and he was snoring gently, and it was another couple of seconds before my body caught up with this knowledge and I felt able to move again.

Cautiously, I opened the cellar door fully and stepped into the entrance hall. From where I stood I could see into the living room and the kitchen, but I could not see my bag anywhere. It might have been hidden in one of the many cupboards that lined the walls, but I doubted it. From the way the Captain had been clutching the bag, it seemed clear that wherever he was, it would be too. There was only one other place to check.

Upstairs.

On tiptoes, I crept along the entrance hall and began to ascend the stairs. The old boards creaked beneath me as I climbed, regardless of how gingerly I placed my feet. Each step I took felt like an eternity as I waited for the sounds to be heard and my presence to be detected.

At last I reached the upstairs landing and surveyed the doors around me. There were three rooms – two that looked like bedrooms and one that looked like a bathroom. Only one room was lit – the bedroom to my right. I moved towards it, crouched down, and put my eye to the keyhole.

There he was.

The Captain was seated at a writing desk with his back to me and on the bed behind him was my bag. He was engaged in writing a letter and on the desk next to his right hand stood a radio which crackled with voices every now and then.

I took a step back and drew in a deep, steadying breath. I could not believe what I was about to do, but I knew I had to do it. I had come too far not to.

I checked through the keyhole one last time – to be sure he was still facing away – then I placed my hand on the door knob, and cautiously entered the room.

As I slipped inside I left the door slightly ajar, in case I needed to flee. The bed was directly ahead of me and I moved towards it as quietly as I could. A blare of static came from the radio and I dropped to the floor at once, my heart pounding like a drum. The Captain, however, seemed unperturbed and continued writing.

From where I lay I could see the Captain's chair legs and his heavy boots, immaculately polished to the point that they reflected the room around them. With little other choice, I crawled on my belly and slid under the bed until I lay prostrate directly behind him.

I shuffled onto my back and took a moment to gather my nerves. I was trembling all over with fear, my hands shaking so badly I was worried I would not be able to grip the bag. My teeth chattered together and I was forced to clamp my mouth shut to silence the noise.

Compose yourself! I thought angrily.

I held my breath and slowly – oh so slowly – slid my hand out from under the bed and reached up towards my bag. My questing fingers found the bedspread and as I felt about I brushed the strap, but just at that moment the squeak of the Captain's chair alerted me to his movement and I whipped my hand back out of sight.

The Captain turned in his seat and reached over to my bag. He picked it up, undid the straps and withdrew the diary, then flung the bag back onto the bed. I bit my knuckles in frustration.

Now what?

Leaning back in his seat, the Captain began to flick through the diary, pausing now and then at entries that interested him. A familiar anger boiled up inside me at the thought of him reading those words that were not meant for him.

I was just trying to figure out a new plan of action when the radio crackled again and a voice – half muffled by static – spoke:

'Sir? Sir, are you there?'

Sitting up quickly, the Captain threw the diary back onto the bag behind him and picked up the receiver.

'What is it?' he asked. 'Make your report.'

'We think one of the prisoners may have escaped, sir,' the voice said, 'but the other prisoners aren't saying anything.'

'Make them,' the Captain hissed back.

Throwing caution to the wind, I reached my hand up again and groped for the bag. My fingers closed upon the strap and I dragged it off the bed, just managing to catch the bag and the diary before they hit the floor.

I thrust the diary back inside the bag then began to wriggle to the opposite side of the bed. Once out from underneath, I got to my feet, put the bag over my shoulders, and crept stealthily towards the doorway.

I was just reaching for the handle when a knife thudded into the doorframe inches from my face. I turned in horror to see the Captain standing tall and staring straight into my eyes.

'I knew I heard something,' he whispered.

Thinking fast, I grabbed a heavy metal candlestick holder from a bookshelf by the door and threw it as hard as I could at the Captain's head, then turned and dashed out of the room, slamming the door behind me.

From within the bedroom I could hear the Captain's pained voice screaming:

'Guards! Guards!'

Footsteps in the entrance hall below told me that one escape route had been cut off. I needed to find another way out.

Looking up, I saw an open hatch to the loft and I jumped for it, my fingers clutching at the edges. Slowly, painfully, I hauled myself upwards as the soldiers' boots pounded on the stairs below. I just managed to make it inside as they reached the landing. I rolled to one side as bullets tore through the flimsy wooden flooring then looked around frantically for an escape route.

Through a nearby window I could see the pale light of dawn and I rushed towards it and wrenched it open. I was very high up, but looking down I spotted a stack of hay bales below. Turning back, I spotted a guard's head appear in the open hatch and knew I had to make a decision quickly. I looked down at the hay bales once more. It was my only chance. I glanced back just as the guard brought the muzzle of a rifle to bear on me and, with no time to lose, I hurled myself out of the window.

I landed hard upon a hay bale and all the breath was knocked out of me. I staggered to my feet and looked up at the window I had just leapt from to see several guards pointing their weapons at me. Bullets ripped into the ground all around my feet.

I turned and fled westward just as alarm calls went up around the camp, and the Kemalan soldiers gave chase…

CHAPTER 17
The Escape

I had never been more terrified in my life. But I had also never been more certain of my actions. As insane as this all was, I knew – without knowing how I knew – that I was doing the right thing. Even as bullets riddled the grass all around me, I did not feel sorry for the choices I had made; only that it had taken me this long to realise I'd had it in me to change who I was all along.

Above the sound of my ragged breathing and the pounding of my footsteps I heard a heart-stopping noise.

Attack dogs.

Their barks and howls were enough to send a chill down my spine and made me force myself on faster than ever. As I ran those fearsome sounds reminded me of something that had slipped my mind in all the commotion; something that I hated myself for forgetting.

Ada.

I had to find Ada!

I did not have much hope that this would work, but I had to try. I put my fingers to my lips and let out a long, piercing whistle – the same whistle that had brought Ada running when I had become separated from her in the forest after my initial escape.

I fell silent and listened, scanning the area all around for any signs of her as I ran, while behind me the shouts and barks grew louder and louder. But she did not appear. To be honest, I was not surprised. What had I expected? She had more than likely moved on by now. Perhaps she had even gone along with Marco and his parents. Maybe now she could live somewhere safe with a family who would love and care for her.

But a part of me would not give up hope – *could not* give up hope – and I whistled again, longer and louder than before. I listened intently, praying for a miracle. And then I heard it. That beloved sound. It was Ada! She was calling to me!

Spurred on by the thought of being reunited, I sprinted onwards and spotted her up ahead. She was standing at the edge of a nearby forest, looking for me, and when she saw me her joyous bark lent new strength to my limbs.

She ran towards me and when we met I paused just long enough to hug her and check she was not injured. Once I was satisfied, I signalled her to follow me, and we continued on westward together.

Dawn had begun to break. Glancing back, I could see the sun appearing above the eastern horizon, spreading colour once more across the darkened earth. I was passing the forest Ada had been sheltering in and all around me the ground was painted in rapidly diminishing shadows, cast by the myriad trees around me.

Up ahead I spotted another shadow, but this one was vast; a huge circular area of darkness, and it took me a couple of seconds to realise that there was nothing nearby that could cast such a shadow.

It was a hole. Some kind of giant crater in the ground.

As I drew nearer it dawned on me that this was not some natural occurrence – it was a quarry. I had not yet reached its edge, but even from this distance it was easy to appreciate the scale of this excavation. It must have taken hundreds of men to dig it and thousands of man hours.

The barking of the dogs was growing steadily louder and I chanced a look back to see how close they were. I wished I hadn't. The dogs had been cut loose and were bearing down on us, while behind them their masters urged them on to attack.

I could not outrun a dog forever. We would have to try to lose them, and the only way I could see to do that was to head into the quarry and pray the dogs did not follow us.

Gasping for breath, I reached the edge and skidded to a stop. The quarry gaped like an open maw before me, filled with shadows and rubble. I found myself marvelling at such an awesome achievement; it is incredible what mankind can achieve when they put their minds to it, and it is unbelievable just how far they will go to get what they want.

As I searched for a way down I took in the layout of the excavation. The quarry was two-tiered – a steep bank in front of me led down to a mid-level and a ramp from there led down to the lowest level. Shadowy forms of buildings, scaffolding and machinery littered both levels, offering up a multitude of escape routes.

By this point the dogs were so close that I could hear their blood-curdling snarls. I turned to see that the two lead dogs were almost upon us, while several more raced after them. I signalled to Ada to follow but she ignored me. She was staring fixedly at the approaching dogs, her teeth drawn back in a vicious snarl and a growl rumbling deep in her throat. I reached over to tug her away by the scruff but she growled at me and I withdrew.

As the dogs finally reached us, I took a step backwards and almost fell into the quarry. But rather than running straight at me, the two lead dogs ignored me completely and headed for Ada.

The first dog charged right at her but she dodged nimbly to one side and it skidded past. The second dog approached more slowly and got within two feet of her before it leapt forwards. Again Ada dodged to one side, but this time, as it passed her, she closed her jaws around its neck and used its own momentum to toss it over the edge of the quarry and down onto the rocks below.

As Ada squared off against the first dog I stepped forwards to help her, but she turned and growled at me as if to say: *Run! I will deal with this!*

I did not know what to do. The other dogs were closing fast and they would tear me to pieces. Feeling helpless and torn and completely forgetting the gun in my bag, I looked down at the steep slope leading to the mid-level… and stepped over the edge.

Rocks and protruding roots tore at me as I slid down the slope and a mini avalanche followed in my wake. I tried to slow myself with my heels as I neared the bottom but it was no use. I reached out to either side, seeking to grab something to halt my progress, but I only succeeded in skinning my palms.

I hit the ground awkwardly and pitched forwards, landing hard on my elbows. I rolled onto my back, wincing with pain, and inspected my injuries. I was bleeding from a multitude of cuts on my arms and legs. My elbows were deeply grazed and covered in grit. I gently brushed off as much as I could, then looked up at the rim of the quarry.

Directly above me I spotted Ada. She was staring down at me, as though checking I was alright, and as soon as she was satisfied she took off running around the lip of the quarry, followed closely by four or five dogs. She was leading them away; leading them away from me.

I had to go after her. The thought of losing her again so soon after finding her was too much for me to bear. I was just getting to my feet to give chase when I heard an ominous growl above me. I turned slowly on the spot and looked upwards.

An attack dog glared down at me, every one of its jagged teeth visible in a ferocious snarl. Its eyes were trained on mine, radiating hunger and malice. It knew one thing and one thing only. Its masters wanted the target dead or captured… and I was the target…

Without taking its eyes off me it began to scramble falteringly down the slope towards me. I did not wait to see if it made it. I took to my heels and ran towards the dirt ramp to the lower level, not caring where I was going, only seeking to put as much distance between us as possible.

As I started down the ramp I glanced behind to see that the dog had made it to the bottom of the slope and was back on my trail. I would need a miracle to outrun this thing. It was like a machine. It did not show a hint of fatigue, even though it had chased me all the way from the farmhouse.

I reached the bottom of the ramp and looked around the lower level for a place to hide… a wall to put my back against… anything.

On the opposite side of the quarry I noticed a ramshackle workmen's hut built against the wall, its roof flush with the middle level. If I could reach that and climb it, I might be able to escape.

I sprinted towards the hut with the dog hot on my heels. My limbs were aching with tiredness and my chest felt tight; my breath coming in short, sharp bursts. I knew I could not keep this pace up much longer, but I was also aware of the consequences of slowing down...

As I neared the hut I put on a burst of speed and fairly ran up the wall, my fingers stretching out desperately for the edge of the roof. I gripped the guttering – praying it would not come loose – and pulled myself upward, but at that moment the dog caught up to me.

It leapt at my scrabbling feet and sank its teeth into my left ankle. I howled in pain and kicked out at the dog with my free foot. I caught it on top of its head once, twice, three times. On the third strike it yelped and let go, dropping back to the ground.

The pain was so excruciating that I felt nauseous, but I forced myself to focus. I had to keep moving. I felt around for a foothold and gained purchase on a window frame. It was enough. I was able to haul myself up onto the roof of the hut and jump onto the floor of the mid-level.

My left sock was becoming damp and I looked down to see that it was stained crimson. I staggered, feeling faint, but managed to recover myself. I moved to the edge and looked down to see what had become of the dog. To my horror, I saw that it was scrabbling up the slope towards me, its eyes alight with murderous fire.

It was relentless! A creature with a singular purpose. *To hunt.*

I spun around. I needed a way out of here, fast! Against the mid-level wall I spotted a scaffolding construction, used by the miners to reach difficult mineral deposits. It looked old and unsafe, but it led all the way to the top of the quarry. It was my best bet.

I ran towards it and began to climb, just as the dog made it onto the mid-level behind me. As I hauled myself hand over hand, the metal supports creaked and groaned under my weight and I began to think that this had not been such a good idea.

I reached a wooden platform and stopped for a short breather. Warily, I glanced down to check on the dog and leapt back in shock, for I was almost face to face with it! The dog was scrambling up the slope next to the scaffolding, wild with desire to catch me. I had to reach the top before it did or there would be no escape!

Suddenly it had become a race.

I climbed faster than I had ever climbed before, heedless of the strain my weight was putting on the aging structure. I reached another platform but as I stretched my arms up for the next handhold, the boards gave way beneath me and I fell backwards. With a strangled yell, I threw out my hands desperately and gripped a crossbeam just in time.

Somehow – I don't know how – I managed to pull myself back onto what remained of the platform and continue the ascent. By this time the dog was a little way ahead of me, but the slope was getting steeper and I could see that it was struggling.

The top was in sight, but even if I made it there, what then? Climb a tree? Stand and fight? Run and hope the dog won't catch me? *What?* I had no idea what I was going to do… or even if I was going to survive this climb…

With my muscles burning, I finally made the top and rolled onto the platform, just as the dog clawed its way over the lip of the quarry. Its chest was rising and falling like bellows as it snorted like an angry bull.

With nowhere to run, and not really knowing what I was doing, I held up my bag defensively as the dog charged towards me. It leapt into the air and knocked me to the ground, tearing at the bag with its vicious teeth.

Fearing for the safety of the diary, I lashed out at the dog and knocked it off me, then thrust my hand inside the bag. My fingers closed around the diary and the pistol and I withdrew both, just as the dog snatched the bag away from me.

Clutching the diary in my free hand, I levelled the pistol at the dog, watching as it savaged the bag then tossed it – with the remainder of my supplies – back into the quarry. Sweat was rolling down my face and I dashed it from my eyes with the back of a hand as my finger tightened on the trigger.

The dog stalked slowly towards me and I was just preparing to fire off a shot when a blur of black and white fur whipped past and barged into it.

Ada!

The two dogs tore at each other ferociously – neither giving any quarter – and soon the ground was stained with blood. I kept the pistol poised, seeking a safe shot at the other dog, but no such opportunity presented itself. I was forced to watch, breathless, as they battled.

At last, Ada came out on top. Her jaws closed around the other dog's neck and she clamped down tightly, squeezing the life out of it. It thrashed and struggled beneath her – trying to break free – but soon its movements slowed, and then stopped altogether. Finally she released it and it crumpled to the ground.

As she limped away from the body I hurried towards her and hugged her tight. But I did not have time to minister to her wounds. We were not safe yet. We had to get as far away from here as possible.

'Come on, Ada,' I whispered. 'Let's keep moving.'

As fast as we were able, we continued on westward – ever westward – towards the next stage of our journey.

CHAPTER 18
The Breaking point

We had been running for about an hour, or at least… it felt like an hour. I was so drained – both mentally and physically – that I had lost track of time. Since leaving the quarry we had not had sight nor sound of our pursuers, but it had seemed prudent to keep running as long as we were able. We had finally reached that point.

The wound on my left ankle sent searing pain up my leg and my head was spinning – my lungs feeling ready to burst – and when I looked over at Ada, I saw that she was doing far worse than I. She was weaving erratically from side to side as she ran, tongue lolling from her mouth. Her wounds had opened further and thick red blood was spilling through her fur.

We had to stop. I could not push her to keep moving any longer. If I did, I risked losing her for good. I scanned the area for a place to hide and spotted a small barn in a nearby field. It was the only form of shelter for miles around, and so we changed course and headed toward it.

As we reached the wall that bordered the field I looked out upon a dreadful scene. A herd of cattle meandered to and fro, chewing grass and watching the world go by, but not all of them had been so lucky. Many lay dead upon the ground, riddled with bullet holes and surrounded by flies.

Something awful had happened here. Either a battle had been waged and these poor creatures had become unwitting casualties, or they had been deliberately used as target practice by bored soldiers looking for a bit of fun. I did not know which one sickened me more.

I averted my gaze as we hopped the wall into the field and followed it round to the back of the barn where a small door let us inside. This was the first chance I'd had to properly rest for hours, but before tending to my own needs I had to see to Ada.

The first thing she did upon entering the barn was flop down on a pile of hay and lie still. She was completely exhausted. I rushed to her side and for the first time I was able to fully appreciate the extent of her wounds. There were deep gashes on her left shoulder and right foreleg and her flank had been torn open by the attack dog's teeth.

Tears sprang to my eyes when it finally sank in that she had taken this punishment *for me*. She had been trying to protect me from harm – suffering the terrible brunt herself – and after all her sacrifices, I had lost the means to treat her. My bag – containing all my supplies and the first aid kit Elsa had given me – were now lying at the bottom of the quarry where the dog had tossed it.

How was I going to help her?

'I'm so sorry, Ada,' I whispered. 'I'm so sorry I got us both into this.'

As the tears continued to fall, I took off my coat, my jumper and my shirt and began to tear the shirt into strips. This was not as easy as it sounds, but anger, grief and shame lent me strength.

Once I had a pile of makeshift bandages, I began to clean the wounds as best I could. Ada licked my hand weakly as I worked and each time she did I felt my chest constrict with emotion.

After I had cleaned away as much blood as possible, I bandaged the wounds tightly. As I looked down at her I felt terrible that I did not have any water to offer. With the amount of blood she had lost, I knew she would be extremely dehydrated.

For the moment there was nothing else I could do for her. With the remaining bandages I cleaned and bound the wound on my left ankle, then moved towards the front of the barn and opened up the double doors that looked out across the field. I was greeted by a sight both forbidding and heartening. Vast seal-grey cloudbanks were amassing in the sky overhead, as though trying to blot out all hope and happiness. In the distance I could see that rain had already started to fall in thick curtains and as I sat there watching, I saw lightning split the sky, followed closely by the rumble of thunder.

As ominous as this all was, it meant there would soon be a plentiful supply of water and I could give Ada the drink she so desperately needed. I did not have long to wait...

Only minutes later the rain came lashing down, beating out a deafening tattoo upon the roof of the barn. The world outside turned dark, as though all colour had leached out of it, and I could hear the cows lowing mournfully as they quickly became soaked through.

Just outside the door, torrents of water poured off the roof and I cupped my hands beneath one of them to catch as much as possible. I conveyed this as carefully as I could over to Ada and encouraged her to lap some of it up. I did this several times until I was satisfied she had drunk enough.

With my clothing drenched, I sat down beside her and stared out across the landscape. I tried to think positively, to reorient my thoughts and renew my sense of purpose, but I had only to look around me to realise that our situation was bleak. The one question that forever plagued me hung tauntingly before my eyes.

'Why am I doing this, Ada?' I whispered, looking over at her. 'Every time I think I've found a reason, I don't seem able to hold onto it... It just keeps on slipping through my fingers...'

I sighed and stroked her neck absentmindedly.

'I'm not sure if I'm doing this because I honestly think it may make a difference, or if I'm just doing it to prove something to myself, I...' I tailed off, unsure how to finish the sentence.

As I looked at Ada – lying still and injured – a memory surfaced; one that I had long repressed and hoped never to recall. It was my deepest, darkest and most shameful secret. I wanted it to remain buried deep in my psyche, but I could not stop the flow of images that danced inside my mind.

It had happened several years ago. As usual, I was spending the afternoon walking alone through the fields outside our village, enjoying the sunshine and solitude. I loved walking alone. It was a chance for me to gather my thoughts, away from the other children who taunted and bullied me.

When I walked the streets of our village, their jeering cries of 'coward' stung me from all sides like a lash, but out here I did not have to bear the brunt of their cruelty. Out here I could relax and, for a few moments at least, let the fear dissipate. Out here was one of the few places I really felt calm... and normal.

A strong wind had started to blow, buffeting me from side to side, and I decided to find a place to shelter until it died down. Across the field ahead of me, I spotted the dilapidated old barn that children from the village often played in. I did not particularly want to meet any of the other children, but it was the only decent shelter to be found, so I set off towards it at a brisk trot.

As I drew closer I heard voices coming from within and I stopped in my tracks. I could hear boys laughing and yelling raucously and I was about to turn around and go search for another shelter, when something stopped me.

Their laughter was not the laughter of excited, joyous young boys, happy to be alive. It was malicious, evil laughter – the kind of laughter only uttered at the expense of another. It sent a chill down my spine and made my breathing quicken. I knew they must be doing something dreadful.

I had to see what it was. I had to pluck up some courage and go and find out what they were up to. But at first my legs would not obey me and I remained where I was. The animal side of my brain was telling me to run, to turn away now and just run. A part of me wanted to heed this warning, but another part of me knew that I couldn't.

For several minutes I stood there – battling my indecision – determined to go and do something, but also determined not to. Finally I broke the spell – the decision made – and forced myself to move.

It was one of the longest walks I can ever remember. Each step seemed like a lifetime as I drew closer to a situation I would normally avoid at all costs. The wind did not help – it tore at my clothing and appeared to be shepherding me along.

In my mind I imagined all the horrible things that could be happening and what the boys might do to me upon discovering them, yet my legs continued to move mechanically, bearing me on into danger.

I reached the barn door and stood still, my heart thumping painfully fast. I had made it this far, but it was not far enough. I needed to push myself that little bit further and find out what was going on.

As though moving in slow motion, I edged my way cautiously along the door towards the opening. I had never been more scared. By this point the animal part of me was screaming inside my head:

Don't get involved – just run!

Turn around now and go!

What are you doing? Get out of there, now!

Somehow I managed to ignore these commands as I reached the opening and peeked into the barn.

At first I thought I had overreacted and for a moment I felt relieved. Perhaps I had misinterpreted the sounds I'd heard. Perhaps my fear-addled brain had imagined the cruel undertones to their laughter – inventing things to be scared of when there was nothing to fear.

What I saw in the barn was a group of young boys standing in a rough circle and looking down at something on the ground. They were probably just playing a game of marbles or kicking a ball around. There was nothing sinister going on here at all.

But then I heard a sound that turned my blood to ice. It was a high-pitched, plaintive mewling and it was coming from the centre of the circle. I saw a boy's leg lash out and heard it connect with something. This was followed by a pain-stricken yelp that was cut short by another boy's kick.

I flinched involuntarily and a gasp escaped my lips. I clapped a hand over my mouth, but it was too late. James Delko, one of the boys closest to me, spun around, breaking the circle and revealing to me the object of their torture. If I was not so scared I would have wept.

It was a small black and white mongrel; a stray I had often seen wandering the fields around our village. It lay prone in the dirt, its right foreleg twisted at a bizarre angle and blood spilling down its sides. They had probably lured it into the barn with food and then trapped it for their dreadful sport. I felt sick to my stomach, but I did not have long to dwell on this.

Delko rushed towards me and grabbed me by the arm, dragging me into the barn to present to the others.

'Looks like we've got a spy, boys,' he said triumphantly, pushing me to the centre of the circle.

'It's just that coward William Belmont,' another boy said, eyeing me nastily.

'What are you doing here, Belmont?' Delko demanded of me. 'Want to join in the fun?'

'No...' I whispered.

'Well, maybe you're here to try and stop our fun,' he continued. 'Is that it?'

'Y... Ye...' I tried to say "yes" but I was too terrified to speak it.

'Cat got your tongue?' he asked. 'Or perhaps the dog?' he added, nodding towards the mongrel.

'Looks like he's about to wet himself,' another boy said. 'Old cowardy Will Belmont.'

'Are you going to go tell on us?' Delko sneered. 'Are you going to go cry to your daddy?'

I could not bring myself to reply. Nothing I could say was going to help my situation. Delko continued to stare at me like I was something nasty on the sole of his shoe.

'Well, here's a reason not to tell on us,' he said, and he hit me in the face. It was not a hard punch, and it did not really hurt, but the shame of it will last forever.

'If you tell anyone what you saw here, you'll get more like that,' he snarled. 'Now get the hell out of here and don't come back.' With that he shoved me hard and I fell to the ground in the doorway. My lip was bleeding and by the time I stood up all the other boys had turned back to the dog, only Delko continued to watch me until I turned and stumbled away.

I had never felt worse in my entire life. Bitter, shameful tears spilled down my cheeks as I rushed blindly towards a nearby copse of trees. All I wanted was to hide. To bury my head in the sand and submerge the shame that tore at my soul.

In that moment I hated myself. I hated how weak I was. How I was unable to stand up for myself. How I couldn't even speak the words I felt, let alone act on them. They had hurt me physically, but the mental scarring of that meeting would last far, far longer.

I reached the edge of the tree line and slumped down at the base of an oak, burying my head in my hands. My body was racked with sobs as the image of the injured mongrel filled my mind. Time slipped away as I sat there and let shame consume every inch of me.

Over half an hour later I heard the sound of laughter in the distance and watched as the boys exited the barn and disappeared across the field.

The dog did not follow them.

I stood up slowly and wiped my eyes and nose on my sleeve. Even as I watched them leave I was still terrified of being discovered, and this only made me loathe myself even more. When I was sure they were gone, I set off towards the barn.

I approached the door slowly and peeked inside. At first I thought the dog must have left without me noticing it, for I could not see it anywhere. My eyes combed the interior, passing over a forlorn little shape by a bale of hay and continuing on. My head snapped back. The shape had moved.

I rushed into the barn and knelt down by the dog. Its right foreleg was definitely broken and it was covered with bumps and cuts that oozed blood upon the floor. It looked up at me with terror in its eyes and tried to crawl away. My heart went out to the poor little creature and I felt repulsed at the actions of those boys.

Just what the hell was going on inside their twisted minds?

I could not answer this question, and in that moment I had no desire to. The only thing that mattered was the waning life that lay before me. I had done nothing to prevent the harm that had befallen this helpless creature, but I would not stand aside and let it die.

I picked up the dog as gently as I could and spoke soothingly to it as I carried it out of the barn and back towards my home. It struggled at first and tried to leap out of my grasp, but it soon settled down. Perhaps it had accepted a fate it deemed inevitable, or perhaps it realised that I meant it no harm. Either way, I eventually arrived home and got down to the business of nursing it back to health.

With my mother's help I was able to get the dog back on its feet within a few weeks, but it was not the same. The dog I had often seen gambolling happily across the fields had died that day.

I named him Milo, and for several months after that dreadful day he was my best friend, and my only real companion. We roamed the fields together every afternoon, hunting imaginary prey and playing fetch; but he was weak, and terrified of everything, and not long after that he passed away. The trauma of his injuries had been too great for him to bear.

I treasure the time I spent with Milo, but the memories of my weakness still haunt me, and always will...

As the memories faded, sinking once more into a place locked deep inside me, I looked down at Ada and saw instead Milo, lying injured upon the barn floor. I had been called coward many times, but that day was the first time I truly called myself it. I had been a coward. I had not stood up for something I believed in, and through my inaction a terrible thing had happened

And it would not happen again.

I stood up resolutely and Ada raised her head to look at me.

'I wasn't sure if I was doing this because I truly believed it would make a difference, or if I was just trying to prove something to myself...' I said slowly. 'Well, I think it's a bit of both. I believe this diary is worth fighting for,' I continued, brandishing the diary at Ada. 'I don't know how I know, and I don't know how it will help, but I do know that it is important, and if I don't do something now, things will only get worse. And – as difficult as it may be – I know I have it in me to overcome my cowardice. I am going to return this diary to Isabella Bertolli, and if nothing else, I will prove that to myself.'

Ada had struggled to her feet and padded over to lick my fingers. I knelt down before her and held her face in my hands.

'We are going to finish this task, Ada,' I said, looking into her eyes. 'You and me together. I know you're tired and I know you're hurting, but I also know that you're strong. We have a long way still to go, so let's keep moving and see where this diary takes us.'

Ada wagged her tail in response and slowly, for she was still unsteady on her feet, I led her out of the barn. The rain had begun to slacken and I could see blue skies through the cloud overhead. Perhaps things were looking up.

CHAPTER 19
The Difficult Decision

Several hours and several miles later, the renewed sense of purpose I had instilled in myself was already beginning to wane. I had not eaten for well over a day. My stomach growled loudly every few minutes and I was starting to feel light-headed. On top of this the rain, which had appeared to be passing over us, had only cleared for around half an hour before starting afresh. Both Ada and I were soaked to the skin and miserable.

My feet ached and I wanted nothing more than to stop and rest, but instead I kept forcing myself forward on our seemingly never-ending westward journey to the Kemalan HQ in Scioli. I glanced at Ada and saw that for all her strength of will, she was flagging badly.

I began to wonder whether we would ever make it to our journey's end, or whether we would be forced to turn back. We had no supplies left; no food or water – *how much longer could we go on like this?* It was all well and good to have noble intentions, but without these basic commodities, intentions – noble or otherwise – would fall by the wayside.

It began to dawn on me then just how alone and isolated I was. I had never been very good at geography and had never bothered learning the layout of our country, and as such I had absolutely no idea where I was. I could be two minutes from the nearest town or two weeks – I had no way of knowing.

This thought brought home a horrible realisation – I could quite easily die out here. I was lost and alone and if I did not speed up – either onwards or backwards – I would starve to death without ever getting to complete my task. At this stage I did not know which one scared me more.

With my mind elsewhere I failed to watch where I was going and my foot caught on something hard and metallic, pitching me forward. I landed flat in a puddle, grazing my hands and elbows, and rolled over at once to see what had tripped me.

It was a railway track!

The track looked newly-built and ran from north to south, but in the distance I could see that it curved to the west. My heart leapt with excitement.

The implications of this discovery were immediately apparent – if I followed the track it would almost certainly lead me to a town. Once there, I could stock up on food and water and medical supplies. I could treat Ada's wounds and my own properly and we could be back on course in no time!

However, my logic was of course flawed – I still had no idea how far away the next town was, and even if I got there, I had no money to pay for anything. And just because I was following a train track, it didn't mean I'd get there any faster. But at the time I was just happy to have something to give me hope.

Feeling more invigorated than I had in days, Ada and I set off along the track. In my mind's eye I pictured the town we would arrive in, and all the food I would eat once we got there…

Two days later we were still following the railway track and the rain continued to pour down. We had not come across any signs of a town and we had neither seen nor heard a train. Our situation was becoming increasingly desperate. I had developed a bad cold – due to being constantly cold and wet – and I had not slept for more than a few minutes in the last three days. When I had slept, I had been sitting uncomfortably at the base of a tree, trying to find rest and shelter where there was none to be found, and if anything, it had only made me feel worse.

But it was Ada I was most concerned for. I had never seen her look this bad. Her tail hung limply between her legs, her nose was dry and her eyes seemed somehow dimmer. And – as hard as it was for me to say it – she was also slowing me down.

I tried to encourage her. I tried to coax her along. I tried to make her realise that if we just sped up a bit, we might soon find warmth and safety and food. But nothing I could say or do would make her go any faster. It seemed that together we were fighting a losing battle and something would have to give, sooner or later...

I decided we should stop and rest so I could take stock of our situation. At least, that was what I told myself. In actuality it was because my stomach was now hurting so much it often forced me to double up in pain. It felt as though I was being eaten from the inside out. I just needed to take a few minutes to try to compose myself.

Through the rain and mist I spotted a structure a short distance ahead of us. It was a railway siding, complete with a shed in which train carriages could be stored. It was the first real shelter we had seen in days and when we saw it we both quickened our pace, pleased at the chance to get out of the rain for a while.

We dashed inside the shed and were enveloped by the thrum of rain beating incessantly upon the roof. We were dripping wet and while Ada shook herself dry and lay down, I tugged off my sodden coat and jumper and wrung them both out upon the floor.

A cold wind blew through the shed, sending a chill throughout my whole body and triggering a sneezing fit that seemed to go on and on. By the time it passed my head was pounding and my eyes were streaming. I sat down beside Ada and rubbed at my red-rimmed eyes.

'Oh, Ada,' I whispered hoarsely. 'What are we going to do?' She raised an eyebrow and glanced up at me, whining softly. I stroked her until she fell silent and I realised she had fallen asleep.

'Good idea,' I muttered. 'Good idea.' It was not a good idea. Yet again I was forgetting the golden rule my father had always taught me on our hunting trips: *Never fall asleep when ill or wounded. Always do whatever you can to treat yourself before considering sleep.* But by then I was past the point of caring. I lay down close to Ada and was soon fast asleep upon the damp floor.

I was awoken by a deep, low rumbling that sent tremors through the ground beneath me. The sound was gradually increasing in volume as the source drew closer and closer. I had experienced this before and knew what it was at once.

Tanks.

I stood up quickly and almost fell back down as blood rushed to my head. I waited a couple of seconds for it to pass, then threw on my jumper and coat and hurried to the door of the shed. I peeked out of cover and at first could not see any sign of the tank.

The rain had abated somewhat but fog now hung over everything. As I strained my eyes to see, I noticed a light drawing nearer and with it the sound grew and grew. Something wasn't right. This did not sound like a tank. It sounded larger. It was only as the light reached me that I realised what it was. It wasn't a tank at all.

It was a train!

The train was moving slowly; passing by our siding and continuing on west. It was our one chance. Our one and only hope of finishing this adventure. I turned and ran towards Ada.

'Ada!' I yelled. 'Ada! We've got to move!' Ada leapt to her feet as though stung by a wasp and looked up at me with nervous, questioning eyes. As I rushed past her towards the other end of the shed, I caught her by the scruff and dragged her up to speed beside me.

We exited the shed together and hurried after the train, quickly drawing alongside it. I scanned the carriages – looking for a way inside – and spotted one up ahead with the door open. I put on a burst of speed I did not think I was capable of and in no time at all was level with the door.

I turned to look for Ada – so I could help her into the carriage first – but to my horror, I saw that she had fallen behind. She was running as fast as she was able, desperate to keep up with me, but a combination of her wounds and fatigue had taken their toll. She would never be able to catch up now...

Unconsciously I began to slow down and the open carriage door drew slowly away from me. It was at that moment that I was forced to make the most difficult decision of my entire life.

Do I get on the train, or not..?

I knew the decision would make or break the task I had set myself, and I knew the decision would likely govern whether I lived or died. But I also knew what making the decision could mean for Ada.

Was I prepared to pay that high a price?

I was beginning to tire. I had to make my decision quickly, but I was torn in two.

I can't... I thought. *I can't just leave her...*

You have to, a firm voice in the back of my head growled. *You know you have to.*

No, no... There has to be another way!

There isn't... You know there isn't.

But she could die! I screamed back at the voice.

And her memory will live on in you forever...

I glanced back at Ada and saw that she had dropped even further behind. With a heavy heart, I turned away, forced myself into a sprint, and caught up to the door once more. I gripped the handle and hesitated one last time, then swung myself inside and knelt in the entrance.

From my vantage point I could just about see her. She was still running after me, still struggling to keep up, and I felt my heart break within me. She slowed to a stop and I could sense the confusion blooming in her eyes.

'I'll come back for you! I promise!' I yelled, but I don't know if she heard. Then the fog swallowed her whole, and she was gone.

I continued to stare after her for several minutes, then slumped back inside the carriage and wept until no more tears would fall. I had never felt more wretched. I had betrayed my faithful companion after she had risked her life for me on multiple occasions. I had sacrificed her for a hare-brained cause of my own creation; a deluded, grandiose notion that what I was striving for might actually mean something.

I was disgusted at myself and ashamed of my ridiculous, self-serving actions. I pulled the diary from my pocket and drew back my arm, prepared to throw the damn thing out of the carriage. Then my grip loosened and my arm fell limply at my side. What good would throwing the diary away do now?

Now that I had put myself in this position, the least I could do was to finish the task I had set myself. I had to find out whether or not it was worth the price I had paid. I doubted whether it would even come close.

Miserably, brokenly, I dragged myself into a corner of the carriage and propped myself up against a wall, the diary still in my hand. I opened it and flicked through to the last entry I had read. *I needed this.* I needed to try and remind myself why I was doing this. I needed to alleviate the sorrow and regret that tore at my soul…

CHAPTER 20
Isabella's Story: Part 3

October 2nd 1942

I had never experienced the life of a prisoner before. I had never understood what it was to have your freedom taken away from you; to have your hopes and dreams shut off from you behind a chain-link fence. I had never known what a strange and frustrating feeling it was to have liberty so close at hand, and yet so far away.

But now I do.

I am looking out across a prison camp. My mother is sitting silently beside me. She has hardly said a word in days. We are surrounded on all sides by the survivors of the terrible attack on our town. I am shocked by how few of them are left. I see some faces I recognise, and also notice the absence of many more.

I find that I am writing now out of a strange mechanical compulsion to do so. Part of me has no desire whatsoever to write, while another part of me still wishes to chronicle what has happened to us in the hope that – one day – someone in power will read this, and realise that this war must end...

It has been eighteen days since my father was killed by the Altegan soldiers, and I still feel the pain of his loss like a dagger in my heart. The grief we felt might have been easier to bear if we had at least been able to mourn his passing properly. But the turn events took after his death meant that we had not even been able to bury him.

The Altegan attack had taken the Kemalans completely unaware. They had managed to defend against it but they had lost many men in the process, and their vicious battle had left the town in ruins. It was now of little use as a strategic outpost or staging area, and as such, the Kemalans no longer needed to stay there.

The battle itself had ended around an hour or so after my father's death. In truth, my mother and I had been completely oblivious to its conclusion. Nothing else in the world had seemed to matter anymore. With difficulty, we had carried my father indoors and laid him on the sofa in the living room. We covered him in a blanket up to his neck and for a moment it had looked as though he was merely sleeping.

And that is the last image I have of him in my mind. Not long after that the Kemalans arrived at our door and forcibly removed us from our home. My mother had been incandescent with rage. She had bit and scratched and lashed out at our captors, trying desperately to break free and return to her husband. But the soldiers had not let her go and we soon found ourselves in the centre of town, surrounded by other survivors.

The Kemalans had scoured the ruins so they could round us up like cattle and gather us in one place. I should have been scared. I should have been terrified about what they were planning to do with us. But all I could see at the time was my father walking bravely towards the Altegans with his rifle in his hands.

'Don't worry, darling,' my mother had said. 'Whatever they have planned for us, we will see your father again – one way or another…'

When the Kemalans were all but certain that they had found everyone, they formed us up into groups – flanked on all sides by armed guards – and marched us hard and fast into the west.

And that is how I came to be in this prison camp.

Right now I am weak with hunger and thirst. We have had no food or water for over two days and I am beginning to feel light-headed and drowsy, even though it is the middle of the day. As horrible as these conditions are, I do not think the soldiers are inflicting them on us deliberately. I have been paying close attention to their activities and I have not seen them eat or drink much either.

I think that our town had a lot of value to them. I think it is where they got most of the supplies they needed to feed the surrounding camps and outposts and its destruction has hit them very hard. They say an army walks on its stomach. Well, it seems that this stomach is empty. I can see it all around me.

The soldiers are quieter than usual, nothing like the rowdy men who until recently had occupied our town. Most of them had been itching for a battle, and now that they had had one, they seemed pale and subdued. I guess that was partly out of hunger, but also because I doubt many of them had ever experienced a battle that brutal before. Most of them look little older than sixteen or seventeen. I wondered whether they had volunteered to fight, or whether they had been drafted against their will.

The mood of the soldiers and my fellow prisoners hangs like a black cloud over the camp. No one speaks much and the only real sound to be heard is that of babies crying. It is an awful, plaintive noise that fills the hearts and minds of everyone close by, intensifying our grief and sorrow. It makes me think about everything I have been through recently. And everything I have lost.

I have seen a lot of terrible things in the past few weeks. I have seen soldiers on both sides commit dreadful acts that would not even enter my worst nightmares. But now and then I also see signs that not all of them are monsters; not all of them are heartless killers.

One such incident occurred only this morning. A small amount of food arrived from a nearby camp and it was immediately distributed among the soldiers for their consumption. Most of the men wolfed down their rations in the blink of an eye, but one man – one of the younger soldiers – hesitated and looked towards our prison pen.

A woman, someone I had seen around the town but never spoken to, was standing by the fence with her young child. The child was bawling his eyes out and the woman was doing the best she could to quiet him down. The soldier stood up slowly, watched by his comrades, and approached the fence.

The woman turned as he approached and the soldier said something to her, but I couldn't hear what it was. He then proceeded to push his rations through the fence into her waiting hands. Then, without a word, he turned and walked back to his fellows. The woman watched him leave silently, then began to feed the rations to her child, who immediately stopped crying.

It is little moments such as this that remind me that they are in fact human. I have demonised them so much in my mind that I often forget this simple fact. In the end, they are just men doing a job, fighting out of honour or duty or even fear. Most of them know nothing of the machinations that go on above them. It is not these men I should direct my anger towards, but the men above them; the men at the very top who turn the cogs of war.

It is these men who have torn my family apart. It is these men who have taken my happy life away from me. It is these men who have ensured that I will never again ride my favourite horse through my father's fields.

I yearn to return to such simple pleasures, but I know that this is a fool's dream. That life is now a million miles away and nothing anyone can do or say will ever put things back to the way they were. My life has changed for good. All I can do now is continue to chronicle my journey into this strange new life, and hope… *believe*, that someday my words will be heard.

I must end this entry here. There appears to be something happening. I think perhaps they are about to move us on. *Where are they going to take us now?*

October 10th 1942

For anyone reading this, I am sorry if you find my words difficult to understand. I am writing this on the move so it is hard to remain legible. My mother and I, along with the rest of the prisoners, are being marched westward once more. I heard one of the guards say that we are heading to the Kemalan HQ in Scioli. I would like to give more information, but unfortunately, I do not know why they are taking us there, or even where Scioli is.

We have been marching for several days now and I no longer have any idea where we are. Earlier this morning, we passed by a village called Chotolo, but I had never heard of it before so it did not help me get my bearings.

The Kemalans have still been unable to give us much food or water and hunger has started to take its toll. Several older prisoners collapsed with fatigue and it was only with the help of those around them that they were able to continue. Everyone is hot and tired and irritable, and the guards have started beating anyone who holds up the group.

Throughout all this my mother has remained silent, and I have become extremely worried about her. There is a distant, faraway look in her eyes and when she looks at me, I do not think she really sees me. I am terrified that my father's death will be too much for her to bear, and I will lose her too...

Wait.

Something's happening.

There is a commotion up ahead. I cannot really see over the heads of the people in front of me, but it looks like the guards are laying into one of the prisoners. Ah. The crowd has parted slightly and I can see that it... it is an elderly man! The guards are kicking him and beating him with their weapons, reminding me of the night my father was caught stealing his own food.

They are trying to force the man to stand back up and join the group, but he is so weak that all he can do is lie there and take their punishment. If they do not stop their assault soon, they will surely kill him!

There are men shouting somewhere behind me, their voices harsh and angry. They are telling the soldiers to stop, but they will not listen. At first I cannot see who is shouting, then five men push past me and rush towards the soldiers. I realise that I recognise some of them. I had often seen them around town when I went with my father on his deliveries.

The soldiers raise their weapons to defend themselves, but they are not fast enough. The men bull them backwards and begin to lay into them with their fists. Their attack is swift and brutal and before anyone can stop it, one of the soldiers lies dead upon the floor, his face a mess of twisted bone. His killer stands up, his fists caked in blood, and I realise that I recognise him too. It is my uncle!

The remaining soldiers continue to fight desperately, yelling for their comrades as loud as they can. A second soldier falls dead under their fierce onslaught, then reinforcements arrive, and the men are subdued.

My hand is shaking so much, I can barely keep writing. The five brave men – who risked so much to save the old man – are now being shackled and led to a ditch at the side of the road. I have witnessed something like this before and I know what it means.

It is a firing squad.

They force the men to kneel on the edge of the ditch, facing away from us. The soldiers who were attacked line up behind them with their rifles at the ready. The men, including my uncle, show no trace of fear. Their backs are straight, their heads held high, their eyes fixed on the horizon.

The battalion leader, the same man who had spoken out against crime – both civilian and military – moves into view and addresses us.

'I told you once that I would not tolerate crime from anyone,' he says loudly. 'And this vicious and unprovoked assault…' Boos and yells of outrage tear from the throat of every prisoner in earshot and I scream along with them.

How dare he say it was unprovoked!

The battalion leader tries to make his voice heard, but soon gives up as the din continues to increase in volume. He signals to the waiting soldiers. It is about to begin.

I must end this entry here.

I must try and do what I can to stop this horrific spectacle.

If anyone ever reads my diary, know this: I would sacrifice *anything* to end this war, and to those of you who would wield power like a toy, I say this to you – the bravest people are often the weakest and most downtrodden…

Here ends the diary of Isabella Bertolli.

Within the bumping, rattling train carriage, I numbly set the diary down upon the floor. The harrowing account I had just read played out vividly in my mind and from that, and what I had already discovered on my own, I was able to piece together what must have happened next.

Isabella must have rushed towards her uncle, desperate to save him from the firing squad. But she will have been too late. The rifles must have been deafening up close, echoing throughout her body and soul. Her uncle and his four brave companions will have crumpled lifelessly into the ditch, where they lay in the mud and filthy water, as their own blood pooled around them.

Isabella – being the courageous person that she is – will have continued on regardless, hoping against hope that her uncle was not dead, but a soldier must have grabbed her before she could reach him. There will have been a scuffle, as Isabella fought to get free so she could tend to her uncle. The diary must have slipped from her pocket, and in the hubbub the soldier must have trodden it deep into the mud.

The soldier will have carried Isabella – kicking and struggling – back to the group and forcibly detained her, whilst the other soldiers organised the remaining prisoners and got the march underway once more.

At least, that is what I hope must have happened. Well… perhaps "hope" is the wrong word. What I mean is, I'd rather not be wrong. For all I know, it could have been very different. Perhaps Isabella had never re-joined the group. Perhaps she had been killed along with her uncle. Perhaps her body had been somewhere by that roadside, and I had simply not seen it.

All these thoughts and more crowded my mind, but for once I decided not to listen to what my head was telling me. In my heart I knew that Isabella was alive. She just had to be. If she had died, I felt as though – somehow – I would have sensed it.

No. She was definitely alive, and I was going to find her.

As I lay back against the wall and tried to fall asleep, Isabella's final words resonated within me: *the bravest people are often the weakest and most downtrodden...* I had always been a weak person; shy and quiet and fearful, but I felt that in the last few days and weeks, I had begun to shrug off the label that had followed me for years. There was no doubt that I had been a coward, but in completing this adventure I hoped to prove to myself, Isabella and the world, that it is possible to change who you are...

CHAPTER 21
The Bridge

The train slammed on its brakes and I jolted awake as the carriages bashed into one another. The force was so violent that I cracked my head off the wall behind me and bit my tongue so hard it bled. Rubbing the back of my head, I looked around the carriage. Something was going on. Either we had reached a station – which seemed unlikely given the suddenness of the braking – or we were being stopped.

I moved towards the carriage door and looked out upon the world. Night had fallen and shadows clung to every bush and tree, but a quarter moon hung high in the sky, bathing the landscape in its pale glow.

We were still moving but we were rapidly slowing, and as I looked towards the front of the train, I saw what was stopping us.

Soldiers.

Lots of them.

In the pale moonlight I could just make out a rail bridge up ahead. The bridge spanned a shallow gorge with a vast, turbulent river at its centre.

Jeeps and tanks were parked across the track and soldiers swarmed around them, armed to the teeth. It appeared to be some kind of checkpoint, and as soon as I thought that, I realised what it meant.

It was an inspection.

Those soldiers would soon board this train and they would check every inch of it before allowing it to travel any further into their territory. If they found me here… I did not like to think what they would do to me, especially if word had reached them about my escape from the prison camp.

I had to get off this train, but it was still moving too fast. Did I dare risk jumping? I was already weak with hunger and fatigue and if I jumped, I was worried it might finish me off. But as we drew closer to the checkpoint, I knew I had no choice.

I left it as long as I could, then lowered my legs over the side of the carriage and braced myself for the impact. I took a couple of deep breaths to steady my nerves… then pushed myself off.

I hit the ground hard and rolled down the bank at the side of the track. Unable to stop myself, I crashed painfully into a bush and was jerked awkwardly to a halt. I lay there for a few seconds, then sat up slowly, flexing my wrists and ankles to make sure that nothing was broken. Apart from a few cuts and bruises, I seemed to be all right.

Cautiously, I peeked out of the bush to check if I had been spotted. As far as I could tell, my presence had not been detected. The train had finally stopped

– its chimney stack still gushing smoke – and one of the soldiers was speaking to the driver. When he was done talking, he signalled to his men and they fanned out to begin their search of the train.

While their backs were turned, I snuck out of hiding and used the cover of some nearby trees to creep closer to the checkpoint, so I would have a better view of the bridge. On several occasions I thought I had been spotted, but at last I reached a safe vantage point on a low rise and was able to survey the area.

It did not look good.

I needed to cross the river to continue my journey and if I was going to do so, I needed to do it now, while the soldiers were distracted by their search. But I could not see any way to get across. The bridge itself was crowded with soldiers and the water looked incredibly fast-flowing – I knew I would be drowned if I tried to swim it.

I needed to find another solution… and quickly.

After looking at the situation from every angle, I had to admit that there was only one other solution, and I did not like the sound of it one bit. If I could not walk over the bridge and I could not swim past it, then the only option left was to climb across it…

I started forward – my mind made up, my purpose clear – when a soldier close by yelled to one of his companions and the spell was broken. I dropped onto my belly and realised that I was breathing fast, on the verge of hyperventilating.

What the hell was I doing?!

The reality of what I was about to attempt struck me then and I could not believe I was even contemplating it. Who the hell did I think I was? I wasn't some comic book action hero. Real people didn't do this sort of thing. Had I gone mad?

I tried to slow my breathing, think rationally and focus while I reassessed my options, but my eyes kept being drawn to the soldiers searching the train. As soon as they were done and they returned to the checkpoint, it would become a whole lot harder to cross the river.

I was fast running out of time and no other options had presented themselves. It was an insane and dangerous plan, but I had to give it a go or risk losing the opportunity. I squared my shoulders and tried to dredge up some self-confidence – *this plan would work!* – but I did not believe myself.

Before I even made it to the underside of the bridge there was another obstacle I would have to navigate first. Their camp. Sleeping tents and aid stations littered the area between me and the river and here and there armed soldiers snoozed or chatted around open fires. It was a veritable minefield, but I would have to get past it if I wanted to reach the bridge.

As quietly as I could, I made my way down off the rise, staying in the cover of any shadows, trees or bushes along the way. I was so nervous that I held my breath the entire time and when I stopped behind a tent, I was forced to take a huge lungful of air to avoid passing out.

I peeked around the side of the tent and quickly withdrew at the sight of three soldiers apparently staring in my direction. I caught my breath. Had they spotted me? When no alarm calls were raised I peered out at them once more and realised, to my relief, that they were all fast asleep where they sat.

After checking there were no other guards nearby, I slunk around the corner of the tent and began to edge my way past the sleeping soldiers. As I passed behind one of them he snorted in his sleep and slumped forward, jerking back up again almost in the same moment. I froze. For a second I thought he must have awoken, but then his gentle snores reached my ears and I breathed a sigh of relief. With renewed caution, I continued on.

Slowly and carefully, I made my way through the camp in this fashion, using whatever cover I could find and biding my time until it was safe to move on.

I was nearing the edge of the camp when I heard a sound that froze the blood in my veins.

The train whistle.

It was getting ready to move on.

The soldiers must have completed their inspection and were allowing the train to continue. In a few moments this sleepy camp would be bustling with life once more. I had run out of time.

Throwing caution to the wind, I broke cover and sprinted towards the bridge. A soldier with his back to me turned at the sound of my passing, but I had ducked out of sight before he was able to get a look at me. I hoped I had not just given the game away.

Breathless and terrified, I finally made it out of the camp and skidded down an incline where I came to a stop behind a rocky outcrop. As I hunkered down to get my breath back, I checked over my shoulder to see if I had been followed. It seemed I had been lucky. No one appeared to be chasing me.

When I felt ready, I got to my feet and quickly surveyed the area. The bridge reared above me, dark and menacing against the night sky, and below me the choppy water roared like a living beast. I had to fight hard to quell the rising terror within as I tried to focus on the task at hand.

The bridge supports were built upon the bank of the river a few feet below me. To climb across I would first need to drop down in order to climb back up again. Above the supports, the underside of the bridge was a lattice of crisscrossed beams and pipes, affording plenty of handholds right along its length. For a moment I began to think that this might just work…

I slid out from cover and approached the edge of the gorge. It was a steep drop to the bank below but, remembering the quarry, I knew I had seen worse. I squatted and began to ease myself down the bank in a controlled slide. Glancing up at the bridge I noticed torch beams sweeping the air and it reminded me that one false move could be fatal.

I was desperate not to make any noise, but every stone I knocked loose in my descent sounded like an avalanche – even above the roar of the river. When I reached the bottom I bent double and ran as fast and as quietly as I could into the shadow of the bridge support.

Once there, I took a moment to steady myself and sized up the climb ahead of me. Up close it did not fill me with confidence. Even at full strength this would push me to my limit but, as it was, I was weak from hunger and tiredness and as though to prove the point, a wave of nausea swept over me.

This was too much.

I must be out of my mind...

Before I knew what I was doing, I had a grasped one of the lower beams in my right hand and begun to haul myself up the support. Achingly slowly, I inched my way higher and higher and within minutes my legs were shaking and my muscles were burning. The wind whipped at my clothes, threatening to drag me back to earth, and I was forced to cling on for grim life.

After what seemed like hours, I reached the top of the support and looked across at the next phase of the climb. The crossbeam structure was arched, meaning that I would have to follow its contours and go higher on the way over. It made me dizzy just thinking about it. I had never had much of a head for heights, and right now it was really putting me to the test.

For a few minutes I just clung there, delaying the inevitable moment when I would have to begin the next phase. But with every passing minute I was wasting precious energy and my weakened left ankle was beginning to shake with fatigue. I just had to grit my teeth and get on with it.

My legs felt like jelly as I stepped onto the crossbeam and began to edge my way across the outside of the arch. I tried not to think about the rushing water below me, but the sounds it made seemed exponentially magnified under the cavernous expanse of the bridge.

I was about halfway across when I made my first big mistake. I reached the apex of the arch and – without knowing why, and after telling myself not to – I glanced down at the river below.

The water looked dark, threatening and infinitely deep. As I stared transfixed, strange shapes emerged amidst the eddies of water. I swore I saw twisted faces laughing up at me and skeletal hands beckoning me down into the depths. It was hypnotic. I could not tear my eyes away.

It was a gust of wind that snapped me back to the present, almost dislodging me in the process. I shuddered and gripped the beam tighter than ever and was just about to continue on when the train began to move. With another loud, piercing whistle, it set off slowly across the bridge. Beneath my hands the metal juddered violently and as the bridge took the full weight of the train, I was almost shaken loose, my teeth clattering together like castanets. Dust and stones rained down on me and just when I felt like I could stand it no longer, the train made it fully across the bridge and continued on westwards, a blast on its whistle echoing off into the distance.

After that ordeal I paused just long enough to collect my wits before continuing on to the other side as fast as I was able.

A short while later I found myself above the opposite bank and began my descent back to earth. By this point my strength was failing me and I did not know how much longer I could carry on.

I was about to find out.

I was just in the middle of a complicated part of the climb when the unexpected happened. I was reaching over to grab a new handhold when a soldier passed beneath me and I made my second big mistake. I looked down again.

The sudden movement below had caught me by surprise and in the act of looking to see what it was, I missed my handhold, overbalanced, and slipped from the beam I was standing on.

For a second or two I was free-falling with the ground rushing up to meet me, then my outstretched hand caught hold of a beam and my arm was almost wrenched from its socket as I swung inwards and collided with the support.

The sound of my fall must have reached the soldier's ears for he spun around and looked straight up at me as he fumbled for his torch. I knew I could not let him see me. If I did, it was all over.

Hanging there by one arm, I patted my coat and felt a now familiar weight; a weight that I had become so used to, I had completely forgotten about it. The pistol.

I drew it from my pocket and aimed it at the soldier. He had found his flashlight and was just bringing both it and his rifle to bear on me when I squeezed the trigger and fired a shot directly into his chest.

The bullet hit him just above the heart and his jacket bloomed crimson. Without a sound, the guard toppled sideways and fell with a splash into the river, where his body was swiftly dragged away by the current.

Yells of alarm drifted on the breeze, drawn by the still echoing gunshot. I had to get out of here quickly. I tucked the pistol back into my pocket and with an effort, gripped the beam with my other hand and began to climb down.

The soldiers were rapidly drawing closer, their torch beams scything through the darkness a little way further up the bank. I managed to get myself a few feet lower down the support before my strength deserted me completely and I dropped like a stone.

I hit the ground awkwardly and felt my already injured ankle twist. The pain was excruciating but I tried to ignore it as I stood up and ran in the opposite direction to the soldiers. With each step I felt red hot pain shooting up my leg and I knew I could not outpace them for long. I drew to a slow, agonising halt and collapsed to the ground. In a last ditch effort, I rolled onto my back, drew out the pistol, and squeezed the trigger over and over at the approaching soldiers. But nothing happened…

I was out of ammo.

This was the end of the line.

The soldiers surrounded me and in the darkness their pitch-black silhouettes were the stuff of nightmares. Their weapons were trained on me as I continued to squeeze the trigger to the hollow sound of *click, click, click...* Then one of the soldiers bent over me, punched me hard on the jaw, and I lost consciousness…

CHAPTER 22
The General

I awoke to the sound of rumbling and rattling and knew at once that I must be on the move. For a second I believed I was back in the train carriage, but then I became aware of murmured voices all around me.

I was not alone...

My eyes snapped open and without bothering to register my surroundings, I immediately leapt to my feet and tried to make a break for it. I had not even moved one step before I was grabbed roughly by two pairs of hands and forced to sit back down on the bench behind me.

'Where the hell do you think you're going, boy?' a voice asked me.

I was still feeling groggy and it took a few moments for my eyes to focus. When they did, I realised where I was, and it all came flooding back to me.

Oh, no...

No, no, no...

I felt my world close in around me. I was seated in the back of an army transport truck surrounded by Kemalan soldiers, each of them in full combat gear and carrying rifles. As I glanced around the interior – lit by the early-morning sun – I noticed the canvas covering was flapping wildly in the wind and I knew we must be moving at a fair pace. My jaw ached and when I raised a hand to feel the bruise, I realised that my wrists were manacled together.

I was well and truly trapped.

Fear began to spread through my body like a poison. The Kemalans had captured me and were now taking me God knows where. They must know I killed that soldier. Perhaps they even knew what happened at the prison camp. They could be taking me to stand in front of a firing squad right now…

This was it. This was the end of my journey. This was how my mission would conclude. I would never get to return the diary to Isabella. I had come all this way for nothing. I had endured pain, grief and suffering for nothing. And I had sacrificed Ada for… for what? For a failed endeavour…

A sense of crushing defeat descended upon me. This was not how it was supposed to end. How could I have come so far only to fail at the last hurdle? For some reason my thoughts flew to my father and I could not help but think how disappointed he must be of his useless, coward of a son.

I slumped back against the wall of the truck and as I did so, I was surprised to feel a familiar object in my coat pocket. The diary! Either the soldiers had not bothered to search me, or they had deemed it harmless and left it where it was.

My heart leapt at the thought that it was still in my possession. The mere closeness of it gave me some small semblance of hope. I felt more confident knowing it was there; more sure of myself, and it gave me the courage to speak.

'Where are we going?' I asked hoarsely.

'To our HQ in Scioli,' a young soldier answered at once. He looked quiet, earnest – not like the others.

'What the hell do you think you're doing, private?' a sergeant sitting opposite me barked fiercely. 'Don't speak to the prisoner. And you,' he added, rounding on me. 'Keep your mouth shut.'

'Are you going to kill me?' I asked, ignoring him completely.

'That hasn't been decided yet,' the private replied. His superior turned on him, his eyes bulging.

'What did I just say?' he roared. 'I'll have you on latrine duties for a week!'

'Sorry, sir, but he deserves to know the truth,' the private answered quietly.

'Right!' the sergeant exploded. 'Latrine duty, two weeks!'

I exchanged a look with the private; a look filled with meaning, before I slumped back against the wall once more and retreated inside my head. As my thoughts twisted and turned, my hand gripped the diary and held it tight. It was the one comforting thing in a situation filled with fear, but I was sure it would not last. Chances were that on arrival at the HQ, I would be stripped and searched and the diary would be taken from me. But I would fight tooth and nail before I would let that happen. If they wanted it, then they would have to work for it…

Sometime later I awoke from a doze and looked blearily out through the fluttering canvas flap at the back of the truck. Night had fallen once more; the truck's rear lights illuminating the road a violent shade of red. We must have been travelling all day.

It suddenly occurred to me – if we were indeed heading towards the Kemalan HQ in Scioli, then chances were I would never have made it had I not been captured. I had run out of food and water and had been virtually starving to death. If I *had* made it across the river without being spotted and still had this far to go… I believe I would have died in the attempt.

Scioli had always been the end-goal of my journey – I just hadn't planned on arriving in this fashion.

I glanced around the inside of the truck and noticed that most of the soldiers appeared to be asleep, their heads slumped on their chests. Did I dare attempt the idea that had just entered my mind? I looked through the canvas flap once more and saw that we were still moving at quite a pace, but that had not stopped me on the train…

Wary of the manacles around my wrists, I got to my feet as quietly as possible and began to shuffle towards the rear of the truck, when a voice stopped me.

'Don't even think about it, son.' I spun around and saw the sergeant staring at me from beneath his heavy brow. His eyes flared angrily and he flicked his gaze at the bench I had just stood up from. I caught his meaning.

I moved back and sat down upon the bench, my eyes never leaving his, my stare just as hard and filled with unspoken rage. When he was certain I wasn't going anywhere, the sergeant stood up, stretched mightily, then stuck his head through the window to the driver's cabin and started speaking to someone.

A few moments later he withdrew and I caught the last few words.

'Two minutes, OK.' A chill ran down my spine. We were almost there. The sergeant began to walk up and down the truck, kicking soldiers' legs as he roused them.

'Wake up all you worthless layabouts, wake up! We'll be arriving at HQ in two minutes.'

Time seemed to drag by and those two minutes soon became an eternity. I did not know what was waiting for me ahead, but I did know that I had almost reached the end of my journey – and what a journey it had been.

The squeal of brakes cut across my thoughts and I felt my stomach turn over. We had arrived.

The truck came to a stop and I heard footsteps crunching on gravel, then voices close by. It appeared that we had been stopped at the outer gate. After a few moments of indistinct talking, I heard footsteps draw around to the back of the truck and the flap was pulled open. A security guard peered in, his hand by his sidearm, as he checked for any suspicious activity. He turned to the driver – who had followed him to the back of the truck – and pointed at me.

'Who's that?' he asked.

'A prisoner we captured at the Salpa rail bridge,' the driver replied. 'The same boy who escaped our prison camp outside Portolo.' The security guard looked at me curiously and nodded as though he had heard of me, then let the flap fall closed.

'OK, you can proceed,' I heard him say. Their footsteps receded, the driver climbed back into the cabin, and the truck rumbled off once more.

As we passed through the base I heard the sounds of training exercises in progress; drill sergeants shouting at subordinates, comrades cheering on comrades, weapons discharging. My pulse quickened. I was right in the belly of the beast, and I had no way out…

The truck came to a stop and the soldiers all around me got to their feet and began to disembark, each of them ignoring me completely. I began to think I had been forgotten about when the young private, who had answered my questions earlier, helped me up and aided my descent from the truck.

Once back on solid earth, he held my arm loosely and began to escort me across the parade ground towards a vast, soulless-looking grey building, lit by spotlights. The only bit of life about it was the Kemalan flag fluttering in the breeze and the snipers patrolling the rooftop, scanning the darkened countryside for any sign of a threat.

As we walked, I took the opportunity to survey the area. From what I could see of the floodlit base, the entire complex appeared to be surrounded by a high perimeter wall, with guard towers at every corner. Barracks, aid stations and firing ranges were set at regimented intervals throughout the space and columns of soldiers marched up and down, performing midnight drills, yelling back chants called out by their superior.

We were drawing closer to the large, grey building and my hands began to shake.

'Where are you taking me?' I asked falteringly.

'The General has asked to see you,' the private replied quietly. 'I don't know why, so don't ask. Just behave yourself, act like you're sorry, and maybe you'll be OK.' At that moment the sergeant from the truck appeared at my other elbow and glared at my escort.

'Everything alright here, private?' he asked.

'Yes, sir – just taking the prisoner to see the General as instructed, sir.'

'Good, good, I'll accompany you,' he replied. As we walked, I tried desperately to stop my hands shaking. I did not want to show any fear in front of this bully of a sergeant.

We entered the building and the sounds of the parade ground faded away to nothing. It was bright and cool inside, and so quiet you could hear a pin drop.

'The General will be up in the War Room,' the sergeant prompted. 'Lead the way, private.'

'Yes, sir.'

I was led throughout the winding, twisting interior of the building – past offices, mess rooms, dining halls and prison cells – until we reached a set of stairs with two guards standing watch at the bottom. The private nodded to them and they stepped aside to allow us access.

By this point my legs were trembling badly, but the private supported me as we climbed the stairs, ensuring that I would not fall. We reached the top and found ourselves on a landing, looking at an elaborately-decorated door. At the sight of it I stopped completely and the private almost bumped into me.

'What's the hold-up?' the sergeant growled from behind us.

'Nothing, sir,' the private replied as he gently chivvied me on.

We moved to the end of the landing and the private leant over and knocked loudly on the door. For a moment there was no answer, then a voice within bade us enter. The private turned the handle, pushed it open and ushered me inside.

The room I found myself in was cavernous and must have taken up much of the first floor of the building. It was lit by electric lights hanging from the ceiling and a strip bulb hung over a vast tabletop map at its centre. Flags, banners and weapons were displayed on every wall and a vast coat of arms hung at the far end. Several guards stood to attention on either side of the room, staring fixedly ahead, so still and quiet that they almost became part of the furniture.

The door shut behind me and my two escorts began to lead me to the opposite end of the room. I felt the eyes of the guards fall upon me as we passed. As we rounded a display case, a desk came into view and I saw a man seated behind it, engrossed in writing a letter. He was dressed in full military regalia and at his shoulder was a shining gold insignia. This, then, was the General…

We stopped in front of the desk and the sergeant stepped forward and saluted, then stood to attention. The General did not look up.

'Sir,' he began, 'we have brought the prisoner you requested to see.' The General continued to write his letter and gave no acknowledgement that he had heard. The silence dragged on for several minutes until the sergeant cleared his throat and tried again.

'Sir? We have…'

'I heard you,' the General cut across him wearily. He finished writing his letter and signed his name, then leant back in his chair, interlaced his fingers, and regarded us silently.

I did not know what I had expected the General to look like, but whatever it was, it was nothing like this. The man seated before me looked to be in his mid-forties, with close-cropped dark hair and serious eyes. The lines on his face were evidence of many years of worry and difficult decisions, and he looked both intelligent and thoughtful.

When he spoke, his voice was calm. There was no trace of anger or malice detectable.

'Tell me again, sergeant, why this boy's activities have become such a hot topic around the base.' The sergeant gave me a sideways glance then launched into his story – or rather, *my* story – which he had clearly rehearsed.

'Well, sir, our intelligence operatives have managed to piece together much of the boy's activities from reports sent by our field units. Several of them came into contact with him over the course of the last few weeks and each report has some very… interesting things to say about him. The first contact with the boy occurred after the skirmish in Chotolo…'

'Ahh yes,' the General interjected. 'A most regrettable incident.'

'Indeed, sir,' the sergeant replied. 'The boy was picked up with a number of other survivors and was being led to one of our camps when he managed to escape during the night. He was chased by the guards but was able to elude them in a forest. The next time any documented contact was had with him was during the air raid on Portolo. One report contains a statement swearing that a boy of his description pulled one of our wounded from the line of fire to safety.'

'Is that true?' the General asked me. I did not answer but I nodded almost imperceptibly. He frowned slightly as he stared into my face, then waved at the sergeant to continue.

'Thank you, sir. The next time he was spotted was near the prison camp outside Portolo, where the workforce is constructing the new road. According to the report he created a diversion to distract the guards, attacked the guard who was left behind, and managed to free the entire workforce before he was captured.'

'Did he, now?...' the General murmured as he considered me. I could have been wrong, but did I detect a hint of admiration in his expression?

'None of the workforce was recaptured, sir,' he continued, and I could not control the little burst of happiness I felt upon hearing this confirmed, 'but the boy was taken to the prison camp and locked up. However, that same night he managed to instigate his escape – seemingly with the help of some other prisoners. We tried to pump them for information after, but they wouldn't tell us anything, sir.' The sergeant paused for breath and the General waited for him to continue.

'During his escape he entered the private rooms of Captain Delarossi, stole back his possessions, and assaulted the Captain. The boy managed to escape the camp, pursued by our attack dogs, but was able to lose them in the old quarry. After that, he dropped off our radars for a while and the next contact we had with him was at the Salpa rail bridge, where he killed one of our men and was caught attempting to flee the scene. And that about brings us up to date, sir,' the sergeant finished.

'It sounds like you've had a busy few weeks,' the General said, 'haven't you, Master…'

'Belmont,' I replied. 'William Belmont.' I did not much feel like playing games. The General leant forward and regarded me thoughtfully.

'Can you explain, Master Belmont, why you did these things? It seems to me that, well… it seems to me that the course you steered led you right… here.'

I stared back at him, holding his gaze, adamant not to tell him why I had come all this way; why I had embarked on this journey. And then it hit me. This *was* it. This *was* the reason I had embarked on this journey – I had just not seen it until now. I had thought my end-goal was to return the diary to Isabella, but that was not it at all. That would not help anyone, and that was not what she wanted…

'Sir, I believe I have been drawn here to give you something,' I began, 'an object I have had in my possession since the start of my journey.' I reached into my coat pocket and the sergeant to my left went for his sidearm.

'Did you search him?' the sergeant yelled at the private.

'I did, sir,' the private replied. 'He had nothing on him except…' Ignoring the weapons trained on me,

I withdrew the diary and held it out to the General. I noticed the sergeant visibly relax.

'Sir, this diary was written by a young girl caught up in the maelstrom of your war. A war that took everything from her, and more. There are words in here intended for your eyes and I believe... I *hope* you will wish to read them... I have travelled a long way to be here and endured a hell of a lot, and it has taken me all this time to realise that *you* were the intended recipient of this diary all along.'

I took a step forward to pass him the diary, but the sergeant threw out a hand and gripped my arm to stop me.

'That's alright, sergeant,' the General said, waving him away. With an uneasy look between us, he released me.

The General stood up and strode around his desk, stopping just in front of me. He raised his hand and took the diary gently from my loose grip, his eyes never leaving mine. He turned the diary over and over in his hands, stroking the worn leather, then looked down at the cover. I saw him mouth the embossed name...

Isabella Bertolli...

The General opened the diary and began to flick slowly through it, his eyes flashing back and forth across each page. He turned and began to pace the room as he read, his footsteps loud on the wooden floor. When he turned back to face me, I watched as his expression went from mild interest, to bemusement, to shock and finally, to shame. I stood by silently, reading along with him in my mind, every precious word memorised.

This is what you always wanted, Isabella, I thought. *This is what you hoped and prayed would happen. I just hope it turns out the way you wanted it to, and I hope I did you proud...*

The General was nearing the end when a piece of paper – the final page of the diary – came loose and fluttered to the ground. The General stopped reading and bent to pick it up. I was just able to read the first line before his hand obscured the writing. It appeared to be a draft of a letter and it read: "To the men or women behind this war." I scoured my memory. I had never seen that page before. Had I missed it? Had it been hidden? What was going on?

I watched as the General read the page, more slowly than the rest of the diary, and I noticed his hands begin to shake, almost imperceptibly. His eyes grew moist as he continued to read and silently he moved back towards his chair and sat down heavily behind his desk. When he had finished he set the diary and the loose page in front of him and began to rub his temples with his right hand. Under his breath, I heard him mutter:

'This war has gone on long enough.'

At that moment there was an urgent knock at the door and a messenger appeared. He scurried the length of the room and stopped in front of the

General's desk, standing to attention. The General did not raise his head.

'Sir, the Altegan army is marching on our base. They will be here in less than half an hour. What are your orders?' The General glanced up and gave me a look I could not quite fathom.

'Do not let our forces attack,' he said softly. 'When they get here, I want you to organise a face-to-face between myself and the Altegan commander. Understood?' The messenger saluted and hurried off.

The General got to his feet and drew the sergeant to one side where he could speak to him quietly. I assume he did not want me to hear what he said next, but if that had been the case he would have moved further away.

'Call a meeting with the Council,' he said in an undertone. 'Once I have finished speaking with the Altegans, we must talk about peace.'

The sergeant's eyes opened wide with shock and at these words I felt my heart leap within me.

I had done it.

Or rather, Isabella and I had done it. The question now was whether those words were just words, or whether they would transform themselves into far-reaching actions that would change the world as we knew it…

CHAPTER 23
A Coward No More

Things happened fast after that. The Kemalans and the Altegans called a meeting of their leaders in Portolo to discuss the possibility of peace. At first it had seemed unlikely, for the Altegans would not accept peace unless their demands were met. But in the end sacrifices were made on both sides, and the end of the war was officially declared.

However, there were several small skirmishes before and after the meeting due to poor communication. While both sides agreed that this was unacceptable, they knew it was an unavoidable part of reining in such vast war machines.

As for me, I was imprisoned for a time while they figured out what to do with me. I had killed a man – *two*, in fact – but it seemed they never traced the other to me. However, to counterbalance this I had also helped bring about the end of the war. I think the General had wanted to let me go at once, but he knew he had to follow the proper protocol.

I spent much of my time in prison speaking with the General, who seemed to have taken a personal interest in me. It took him a while to earn my trust, but when he did I relayed to him the entire story of my adventures, only leaving out details of the first man I killed to avoid further complicating my situation. There were parts I found difficult to speak of, but he was incredibly patient and allowed me as much time as I needed to get through the rough patches.

After several weeks of this, I was at last released on a technicality – I was a minor and as such could not be tried in the same way an adult would be for my crimes. I think the General bent the rules a bit on this point, but thankfully no one argued with him.

On the day I was released, the General came to see me once more and handed me back the diary. I was a little surprised at this, but pleased nonetheless.

'You don't want to keep it?' I asked him, as I gratefully accepted it.

'I don't need to, son,' he replied. 'I've got all the words stored up here,' and he tapped his temple. 'Anyway, it's going to be your job to bear it on the final stage of its journey.'

'What do you mean?' I asked.

'You'll see,' he replied cannily. 'You've heard of the Peace Parade they're throwing in Portolo this Saturday?'

'Yes..?'

'Well, make sure you're standing by the King's Monument at midday.'

'Why?' I asked guardedly.

'Just be there,' the General answered. 'My men will escort you to Portolo and set you up in a hotel. You'll be comfortable enough there until Saturday.'

'But what happens on Saturday?' I asked, beginning to get nervous. The General smiled but did not answer as he turned and walked away.

The journey back to Portolo was long and uneventful. I spent much of the time spying for places I had seen during my adventure. We passed the Salpa rail bridge, the quarry, the prison camp, and even drove along the section of road I had seen the workforce constructing.

Eventually we arrived in Portolo and I remembered with a shock the devastation the air raid had caused. But I was pleased to see that it had not dampened the Portolan spirit. Busy people continued to bustle to and fro, and builders were hard at work repairing the damage, while here and there children and their parents hung flags and banners, ready for Saturday's celebration.

I was escorted to my hotel room by a couple of Kemalan soldiers, one of which was the young private, and he reminded me to be at the monument at midday on Saturday. I asked if he knew what this was all about, but he merely winked and said, 'You'll find out.'

It was Friday morning, so I had an entire day to kill. I set off into the town centre and had a wander around, reminding myself of all the places Marco and I had seen the last time we were here. Seeing these places again made me wonder what had become of Marco, and whether he and his parents were alright.

I walked to the cathedral – where the field hospital had been – to see if Elsa still worked there, but when I arrived I discovered that the hospital had been packed up and there was no sign it had ever been there. I felt my heart sink. It would have been nice to see her again.

I returned to my hotel that evening, tired and lonely, and nervous at what the following day would bring. I did not know what the General had up his sleeve, but I did not have too much longer to wait.

The next day dawned bright and clear and when I looked out of my window, I saw that the street was a hive of activity. People rushed here and there, hanging bunting, laying tables and generally setting up, ready for the parade.

I got myself dressed and headed out to see what I could do to help. I ended up joining an elderly couple who were preparing a refreshments point. I helped set up the table, assemble the tea and coffee dispensers and lay out the cups and saucers.

I became so wrapped up in my tasks that when I next looked at the town clock, I saw that it was already ten to twelve. The parade was about to start and I had a meeting to get to. I said my farewells to the couple and hurried off to the monument.

I arrived there just as the parade started and sat down on one of the stairs to watch. I was incredibly nervous. Whatever the General had organised was about to happen, and I still had no idea what to expect.

Twelve o'clock came and went as I watched the dancers, floats and other performers pass by in a rainbow whirl of colour and song. It was a joy to watch, but I got just as much pleasure from watching the audience as the parade itself. Everyone had a smile on their face. Everyone was cheerful. Everyone sang along with the songs. In many minds – particularly the youngest – the war was already receding into memory, and it made me glad to witness it.

By twelve-thirty I began to wonder if the General had been pulling my leg. I was just on the verge of leaving the monument to find some food when I noticed a girl watching me. She looked to be about my age – perhaps a bit younger – and although I had never seen her before, I felt, somehow, like I knew her.

A woman stood behind her, presumably her mother, and she too was watching me. For a moment we just stood there, looking at each other, then the girl approached me. She wore a pretty blue dress. Her hair was dark and done in curls that framed her doll-like face. In many respects she looked like any other girl her age, but it was her eyes that set her apart. They were dark green in colour and I saw within them none of the innocence her exterior exuded.

These were eyes that had seen many terrible things; the eyes of a girl forced to grow up too quickly.

She stopped in front of me and continued to stare at me searchingly. Then she spoke.

'William Belmont?' she asked.

'Isabella Bertolli,' I replied.

Half an hour later, Isabella, her mother and I, were seated on a bench a short distance from the monument. There was so much I wanted to say to Isabella that I did not know where to begin, but it turned out that the General had filled her in on much of my adventures.

Instead, I asked to know what had happened to her, and I discovered that she and the rest of the prisoners had been released a few days ago with a full apology from the Kemalan government. The General himself had explained the situation to Isabella and her mother and instructed them to go to the monument where they would meet me.

'The General said that you had something for me,' Isabella said. 'And I think I know what it must be.' I reached into my pocket and pulled out the diary. As I looked at its worn surface, I thought about everything I had gone through to return it, and how much I had changed because of it.

'I've come a very long way to give this to you,' I said slowly. 'And it has affected me deeply. I am not the same person I was when I first picked up this diary. Your words inspired me and drove me;

drove me to realise that I could change – that I did not have to remain a coward all my life.' I held out the diary and Isabella took it. Her fingers traced the spine, welcoming an old friend she thought she had lost. For a time, she was quiet as she reacquainted herself with her possession, then she spoke.

'If even half the accounts I have heard of your exploits are true, then I think it is safe to say that you are a coward no more, William Belmont. From the very start of this war, all I wanted was for my words to be heard by someone in power… and you made that happen. Your adventure has proven that a person can change, and with it, the future of entire nations.'

We sat for several minutes after that and watched the parade in silence. Then I remembered something I had been meaning to ask her.

'When the General was reading your diary, the final page came loose and fell. I hadn't seen it before, but it looked like the draft of a letter, and when he read it, I think… I think that was what swayed him.' I had been looking at the ground, but now I turned and stared into her eyes. 'I think he must have kept it, so I have to ask – what did it say?'

Isabella looked thoughtful for a minute, and then it seemed to come back to her.

'Yes, I… I remember that letter. I wrote it right after my father…' She stopped for a second as she thought back to that night, then she continued. 'I never expected anyone to read it. To be honest, I wasn't even sure I would survive the night, but… it was written to the men or women behind the war, and it said, *"If the world is like a body, then your war is like a cancer. And, like a cancer, if left unchecked, it will grow and spread and consume all in its path. Your war has already done so much damage, the cancer has already scarred this world deeply, and it has been felt by every one of us. It can be seen in every broken family, every wasted life, every ruined town. You know deep down what you must do, and though sacrifices must be made, the cancer must be stopped here. It must be stopped now, or soon there will be no world left to fight for."*

I slumped back and let out a long, deep breath.

'Thank you,' I whispered. 'Thank you.'

We continued to watch the parade for another half an hour, none of us saying anything, until Isabella's mother's voice cut across our thoughts.

'Ah, here they are! Right on time, just like the General said.' I looked up but could not see anyone.

'Here who are?' I asked.

'Some people I think you'll recognise,' she replied with a smile. I scanned the crowd but could not see anyone… and then I saw them. They were walking down the street towards us and I stood up shakily at the sight of them. I had thought I would never see them again, but there they were.

Elsa, Marco and his parents strode towards us and I ran over to embrace each of them. Marco was ecstatic and rattled off question after question that I did my best to answer. When at last he ran out of steam, I approached Elsa and looked up at her.

'I'm happy to see you again,' I said.

'And I'm happy to see you safe and sound,' she replied with a smile. 'I still can't believe I let you walk off after that air raid, but if I hadn't, then I guess that none of this,' and she indicated the parade, 'would have happened. Anyway, I'm not going to let you run off like that again. The General has given me custody of you, and you are to come and live with me. That is, of course… if you want to?'

My eyes lit up and I threw myself at Elsa and hugged her tight.

'I'll take that as a "yes" then, shall I?' she said with a laugh.

A few months later, I found myself wandering the woods and fields around Portolo. I had been doing this a lot recently and was beginning to give up hope. To be honest, there had not been much hope to begin with, but I had not let that stop me. I had to at least try. I owed her that much.

As I walked, I called her name and before long my voice grew hoarse. Night was drawing on and I knew I would have to turn back soon and head home. I was passing a forest and I let out one last desperate yell, as loud and long as I could.

'Ada!'

I waited, listening intently, imagining hearing her beloved reply. It was so crystal clear in my mind that it sounded as though I was really hearing it. I stopped moving. Had I just heard her?

'Ada!' I yelled again. This time I definitely heard something. It was coming from the forest and I rushed towards it. Up ahead, I heard the snapping of twigs as something hurried in my direction. I skidded to a stop as a shape emerged from the tree line and stopped to watch me.

'Is that you, Ada?' I called uncertainly. The shape moved into a shaft of moonlight. I could not believe my eyes. I thought I must have been dreaming. It was Ada! I dropped to my knees in jubilation and opened my arms to welcome her, but she did not rush over to greet me.

'Oh, Ada,' I said brokenly. 'I'm so sorry for what I did. I'm so sorry that I left you behind, but I had to! If I hadn't, then the war might not have ended. We all have to make sacrifices in this world and… and you were mine. Can you ever forgive me?'

Ada looked away from me and for a second I thought she was about to turn tail and run back into the forest. But then she let out an excited bark and sprinted toward me. She ran right into my waiting arms and I held her tight and kissed the top of her head.

'I'll never let you go again,' I whispered as she licked my face. 'The next journey we'll finish together.'

EPILOGUE

One year later, William Belmont stood in the graveyard with his faithful companion Ada by his side. At his feet were two graves, both alive with beautiful wildflowers. The tombstones commemorated the lives of his parents; lives of love, happiness, and – ultimately – sacrifice.

Will had just finished relating the story of his adventures. It had been an emotional journey for him, and he had not been ashamed to let a few tears fall along the way. Now he had reached its conclusion, he did not have much left to say.

'Before I go, I just wanted to tell you about my life now,' he began. 'I have been fostered by a wonderful woman called Elsa Leoni, who you'll remember from my story. She has been incredibly kind to me and has taken me in at her home in Portolo. Marco and his parents live just down the street – I see Marco every day, he is just as loud and irrepressible as ever! Isabella and her mother live the next street over. They are very happy there – Isabella still writes every day and there are rumours that her diary will be published. I believe the General has put in a good word for her, but I am sure he would not say if he had. Also, I have not told anyone this, but... I have fallen in love with Isabella and plan to ask her to marry me someday. I hope she will say yes, and I hope I have your blessing to do so. I have never felt this way about anyone before.' Will fell silent as he stared down at the graves, then glanced behind him at the figures standing nearby.

'I have to go now, but I want to say one last thing. I want to thank you for everything you did for me. I want to thank you for all the love you showed me throughout my life and for the bravery you showed when you gave your lives for me. There is no possible way I can ever thank you enough, but what I can do is try to live my life the way you always wanted me to. I will live my life to its fullest. I will seize the opportunities laid before me. But most of all – although I know fear will always walk with me – I will no longer let it control me.' Will bent down and laid a hand upon each tombstone.

'I love you both with all my heart and you will never leave my thoughts.' He turned then and strode back towards the waiting group – a group composed of Elsa, Marco, his parents, Isabella and her mother.

'Did you say what you came to say?' Elsa asked him.

'I did,' he said thickly.

'Then let's go home,' she replied, and together they headed off towards the town as the sun sank in the distance and set the clouds ablaze.

The Hirono Chronicles: Meera
ISBN: 978-1-913359-98-0

The Hirono Chronicles: Wolf Warriors
ISBN: 978-1-913802-16-5

ALSO BY T.J.H. BOGGIS AND AVAILABLE FROM MARKOSIA

The Hirono Chronicles: Spirit War
ISBN: 978-1-913802-62-2

www.markosia.com